How To Ruin
The Perfect Child

How To Ruin The Perfect Child

Antonio Le Mons

Writes Club Press

San Jose New York Lincoln Shanghai

How To Ruin The Perfect Child

Writers Club Press
an imprint of iUniverse.com, Inc.

For information address:
iUniverse.com, Inc.
5220 S 16th, Ste. 200
Lincoln, NE 68512
www.iuniverse.com

Cover Design by Manuel Diva, Author's Photograph by
Whitney Stolich

Cover Photograph by Jonnie Mills, Digital Imagery® copyright 1999
PhotoDisc, Inc.

ISBN: 0-595-12870-X

Printed in the United States of America

For

My mother, Beverly J. Le Mons

In Loving Memory of

Reginald D. Banks
Thomas Twitty, Jr.
Leopold Clarke
Bobby DeBarge
Markus Collins
Rodney Baxter
Mark Nelson
Parris Gill
Oba

If I cannot share with you
the truth of my existence,
how can you know or love me,
and most importantly
how can you work for freedom
on my behalf ?

—bell hooks

Acknowledgements

This book could not have been written without the love and support of the wonderful people in my life.

To my family: Mom for always believing in me and giving me the freedom to make my own way. Dad for having the courage to give us another chance. GaGa for your prayers and never forgetting to tell me that you love me. Darlene for being hands-down my biggest fan. Twitty for his humor, courage and gentleness. Lee for spending the time. Carl for stepping in. Faye for her never-ending kindness. Kitrina for continually being there for me—I'll owe you for life! Marcos for considering me the best thing next to Playstation 2—I love you guy! Tracy, Tasha, Darren, Mookie and Natalie for all the fun we shared growing up. Maurio for his admiration and unconditional love. Mina for not getting too mad when I call, "just to get Maurio's new number." ShaRon & Brent and Pat & Bob for giving me weekend refuge from the girls. Janet for the cultural education, and having the good sense to know that it's perfectly all right for boys to bake cookies too! Uncle Ernest for the road trip to California in the summer of '77—it changed everything!

To my first-class friends: Bruce for helping me to understand the rewards of emotional expression. Butler for your warmth and sheer goodness (OXOXO). Dana for your boundless humor. Darren for the whole thing (thanks for being the best brista in the world!) Dei Dei for seeing the very best in me. Jimmie for being the consummate host in '86 and a first-rate friend ever since. Kirby for your drive and allowing me to feed off it (man you're going right to the top!). Melvin for your affirmation, your love and free medical counsel. Silvia for your sincerity and kindness. Stephanie for having faith in me and my work. Su & Shelly for your trust! Vicki for your ceaseless love and the afternoon tête-à-têtes over lattes at Starbucks. Ava C, Brent (BJ), Darryl G, David C, David D, Eric M, Francesca M, Jonathan S, Johnny K, Julie A, W, Lisa L/J, Lo, Lyndon V, Marvin J, Michael B, Michael L, Michael P, Michelle F, Nazila H, Ramon V, Rudy C, Scooter, Scotty C, Shonda H, and Woody for your unending friendship, inspiration and support. And to my through it all #1 friend Keith, thanks for everything!— Ours is a friendship Millenniums ahead of its time.

To my contemporaries whom I admire and respect: Jeff Bailey, Bishop Carl Bean, Belasco, Alan Bell, Duane Bremond, Windell Carmichael, Charlene Cochran, Stanley Bennett Clay, Mark Durham, Shawn Hinds, Varnette Honeywood, Cleo Manago, Jonathan Poullard, Kimberly Q, Reginald Smith, George Stallings Jr., Blaine Teamer

(Kudos!), Russ Toth, Jeffery Weddington, Tom West, Phill Wilson, and Roberta Wilson.

To Mrs. Davis, Mr. Jenkins, Mrs. Gamble, Mrs. Perryman, Mr. Duke, and Mr. Brown for a great foundation; Ruth Wolson for listening to endless excerpts from *How To Ruin The Perfect Child* during our sessions; and Wanda, Silvia, and Mrs. Carey, three women who never forget my birthday.

To my editors, Robert Gaylord and Phaedra Torres; my ultra-talented cover designer, Manuel Diva; and my proofreaders, Toia T and the others whose names have been previously mentioned—thank you, thank you, thank you!

And finally to Frederick, the person who makes my heart sing so loud that you can hear it way up in the cheap seats. Thank you for believing in me, encouraging me, and pushing me to finish this book. I love you!

How to Ruin
the Perfect Child

The Beginning of the End

Relaxed and determined, Aprielle entered the reception area with a group of men in dark coveralls. There were no insignias on the coveralls to indicate where the men were from, but Pebbles recognized Aprielle right away, from the dedication photo of her hanging on the adjacent wall.

"Break it down!" Aprielle demanded, pointing the men in the direction of Dr. Hamilton's office. "On three, gentlemen. One...two—"

"Wait!" Pebbles screamed, scurrying to get between the men and the door. "Can I be of some assistance?" she asked, stunned by Aprielle's desire to break into her son's office.

"Who are you?" Aprielle replied. "Pebbles Sinclair, the Center's Administrator," she said, worming herself from behind the man who, as a result of her attempt to stop him, had her pressed against the door.

Pebbles extended her hand. Aprielle carefully scanned her while the men silently looked on. "Administrator?

Really! One would never know," Aprielle retorted, ignoring Pebbles' gesture.

Pebbles had big blonde hair and even bigger boobs that she unnecessarily accentuated. She was wearing a low-cut blouse that revealed just about everything and a mini-skirt that just barely qualified as a skirt and not a headband. She looked more like a Snap-On Tool pin-up girl than she did an office worker.

"Oh this," Pebbles blushed. "We're closed today, so I came casual."

"Casual? I see," Aprielle replied, sarcastically.

Rico, the man who had had Pebbles pinned against the door, flashed her a polite smile while the others snickered and exchanged high-fives.

"Enough of this nonsense," Aprielle said, pushing her way in front of Rico. "Do you have the key to my son's office?"

"I'm afraid I went right off and left my keys laying on the bureau at home." Pebbles smiled to herself at her absent-mindedness. "But not to worry, Dr. Fitzgerald is here. He has a key."

They waited while Pebbles called Dr. Fitzgerald who was the only doctor there. The others, doctors Hamilton, Klein, Ellis and their assistants, were all in Delhi at a wellness conference.

Dr. Fitzgerald's lack of interest in wellness had dictated that he be the one to stay behind to handle patient emergencies.

After a few minutes, Dr. Fitzgerald entered the reception area. He became instantly agitated when he spotted Aprielle. "What in the hell are you doing here, and who are these men?" he insisted, his tone making it clear that she had no business there.

Aprielle stared at him, as she tried to discern what turned her stomach more: the sheer sight of him, or his overindulgence in cheap cologne. Without raising her voice above a whisper, she said, "If you have the key to this door—open it!"

Dr. Fitzgerald hesitated, thinking, "who does this old bitch think she is coming in here demanding anything? There is only one set of cajones here, and she is obviously mistaken about where they are hanging."

It was unmistakable that there was no love between them; their hatred dated back to the merger between her son's pediatric center and his medical group, which she had fought vehemently to stop.

The Maximillian P. Hamilton Riverfront Pediatric Center, as it had been originally called, had been a gift from her for his finishing at the top of his class.

In her determination to see to it that he went straight to the top of the medical community, she had had the illustrious complex erected on a man-made island just off the shore of the Detroit River. She'd even hosted a lavish who's who opening reception.

Prior to the merger, the facility had already been the toast of the community, boasting an unparalleled staff of international holistic professionals, and a breathtaking view of Canada's shoreline.

Its aesthetics and impeccable credentials had made it the desired destination of every progressive pediatric intern in the country.

Its popularity with both parents and children alike had kept the new-patient waiting list consistently filled two years out. Of course, the children hadn't been attracted to the facility's reputation. They loved it for the merry-go-round, state of the art computer toys, and winter ice-skating. Aprielle had managed to get several toy manufacturers to make the facility an official beta-testing site.

Maximillian and his hand-picked team of doctors had been single-handedly pioneering the field of pediatric medicine, treating children holistically, thus sparing their young systems from the eventual results of the overuse of antibiotics and scores of mood altering drugs that were commonly being dispensed.

Maximillian's health and wellness philosophy and his revolutionary approach to medical care had gotten the attention of scores of medical groups. He had frequently been approached with merger deals, but it hadn't been until the Fitzgerald and Klein deal that he'd actually considered it. His lack of interest in a merger up until that point had not been due to a desire to retain a stronghold on the work; he knew that few physicians trained in the United States could truly get beyond the American Medical Association's traditional ideologies to fully embrace his methods. Besides, Aprielle had controlled the board and she had seen no sound reason for him to join forces with anyone, when he could be in command of it all.

Maximillian and Dr. Klein had met while in Australia on business. They had become friendly and had spent a considerable amount of time discussing the future of healthcare. Dr. Klein had become obsessed with Maximillian's prevention and wellness vision and wanted in. Their initial meeting had been followed by several additional meetings, after which Dr. Klein had become convinced that he needed to transform his practice, Fitzgerald-Klein Medical Center, from a back-end treatment oriented practice into a front-end preventive one. His partner Dr. Fitzgerald, however, had been of the opinion, "If it wasn't broken, why fix it?"

Fitzgerald-Klein had also enjoyed a stellar reputation, an impressive clientele and had been extremely profitable. Dr. Fitzgerald had not been interested in tampering with a formula that had obviously been working. But, after months of Klein's nonstop lobbying, he had finally conceded.

Dr. Klein had convinced him that a merger with Maximillian's center was the key not only to their future, but the future of healthcare as well.

The merger, as Dr. Klein had described it, would enable them to expand their client base to include both adults and children, and lay the foundation for full service wellness centers in metropolitan areas throughout the country.

Dr. Fitzgerald hadn't been particularly sold on the whole wellness thing; however, he had seen the enormous profit potential in nationwide centers, and if Hamilton and Klein thought that they could get others to buy into it and he'd make money, which had ultimately been his bottom line, why not?

The moment Fitzgerald had looked as if he'd give in, Dr. Klein had been on the phone to Maximillian about putting together a deal.

Aprielle had become livid when she found out about Maximillian's merger plans. Although Dr. Klein had seemed sincere in sharing her son's vision, she had been certain that Fitzgerald wasn't to be trusted no farther that he could be seen. She had maintained that Fitzgerald and Klein would undoubtedly be the true winners in the deal.

During the negotiations, things had gotten particularly nasty. Dr. Fitzgerald had been against Aprielle from the word "go". The facility had been renamed, The Riverfront Wellness Complex, which in her view had been the ultimate insult to all of her hard work.

When it was all said and done, Fitzgerald had managed to successfully get Aprielle's direct involvement in the center's operations eliminated, on the grounds that she lacked a medical background—holistic or otherwise. However, his attempts to completely isolate her had been unsuccessful. After all, she did own the facility; a fact that he was reminded of each morning as he passed what he thought to be a god-awful photo of her hanging in the lobby.

Dr. Fitzgerald's hesitation to immediately open the door infuriated her. She turned to the men and politely said, "Break the son of a bitch down!"

"That's not necessary," Fitzgerald said, moving towards the door. "Maximillian is not going to like this. You continue to make this transition unnecessarily uncomfortable. You agreed to back off, so why don't you?"

"I do not know what you are up to Fitzgerald, but when I figure it out—and I most certainly will—you had better…"

Her statement was interrupted by a fowl odor that rushed from the room, knocking everyone back.

Pebbles, who had been silently taking in the drama, was immediately reminded of the previous day's events: the children's complaints about a bad smell of which no one could establish the source, and the odd phone call, inquiring about doctors Hamilton, Ellis and Klein's exact whereabouts in Delhi.

Dr. Camille Ellis, although married to Maximillian, never used her married name professionally. She occasionally used Ellis-Hamilton socially, but never Hamilton alone. She preferred the autonomy that her maiden name gave her. Besides, she felt that one Mrs. Hamilton and one Dr. Hamilton in the family was more than enough.

Camille and Maximillian's storybook marriage had become fragile over the past year, primarily due to her unremitting accusations that he was having an affair with his assistant. His refusal to fire the assistant was confirmation to her that her accusations were indeed true.

Maximillian was surprised at his wife's sudden insecurity. They had been sweethearts since medical school, and had never had issues around infidelity. He began wondering if she was the one seeing someone and projecting her guilt onto him.

He believed that theirs was a strong marriage, built on trust and good communication. He genuinely loved her and was more disappointed and hurt than angry about their current impasse.

If Camille had approached him and articulated her concerns, he could have been indulgent, but to out-and-out accuse him of something so unspeakable, not only cast doubt on his principles, it questioned his integrity and the very commitment to her that he so deeply respected.

Although they still lived and worked under the same roofs, they were practically living separate lives, no longer sharing the same bed at medical conferences or at home.

Pebbles knew something horrible was about to be revealed. She could feel it. While everyone else collected themselves, Aprielle marched right into the office.

There was no visible disturbance or evidence of the odor's source, but the strength of it confirmed that there was a problem.

Aprielle took a handkerchief from her purse, covered her nose, and proceeded to the door in the back corner of the room that read "PRIVATE". She turned the knob—locked! "Where's the key to this door?" she demanded.

Dr. Fitzgerald, who was still in the hall, entered the room slowly, moving apprehensively toward the door. Without warning, he was on his knees vomiting uncontrollably. Aprielle, having exhausted all patience, went to

Fitzgerald, snatched the keys from him and pitched them to Rico, who opened the door and lead the group down the narrow hall.

There was a small bathroom to the right—empty! The hall led to a posh sitting area, airy and quaint. The furnishings were expensive but sparse. There was nothing visibly disturbed in this room either, but the odor was much stronger. There was another hall to the right. Rico headed down the hall, Aprielle on his heels and the others following, including Pebbles who looked like she might lose it any minute.

When he opened the door, one of the men fainted, hitting the floor hard. You would have thought that he had seen something, which wasn't possible, given that the room was pitch black. He had apparently been overcome by the odor, which had become suffocating.

Rico felt for the light switch and flipped it on. Pebbles screamed like a live cat being skinned, making the hair on Rico's neck stand. He attempted to cover Aprielle's eyes, but it was too late. The horrific picture had already been registered and etched.

The room resembled a slaughterhouse. Blood was everywhere. Maximillian's body lay face up on the floor, his brains splattered on the wall behind him. His partially clothed assistant Paul lay near him in a pool of dried blood. There was a leather book wedged under Maximillian's body and a small caliber gun in his left hand.

"Get them out of here!" Rico said, referring to Aprielle and Pebbles.

Pebbles was stretched out on the floor whimpering like a wounded animal, as tears flowed slowly down Aprielle's face.

One of the men picked Pebbles up and carried her out, while another tried unsuccessfully to aid Aprielle, who was frozen stiff, clutching her pocketbook. Rico motioned to the guy to let her be, as he quickly removed the leather book from beneath Maximillian's body. After successfully slipping the book into his coveralls, unnoticed, he went to Aprielle and took her gently by the arm. "Mrs. H, it's me Rico. Come on, let me take you home," he said softly. Without a word, she collapsed against him like a rag doll.

Rico escorted Aprielle down the corridor to the reception area, where Pebbles was being fanned and Dr. Fitzgerald was still trying to recover. He instructed Dr. Fitzgerald to call the police and to be sure not to touch anything.

Aprielle walked slowly over to Dr. Fitzgerald and stared directly into his eyes. She didn't say anything, but if looks could kill, he would have been casualty number three.

Chapter 1

"Here Gabby, take this," Rico said, handing me Maximillian's journal from the bib of his coveralls. I recognized it right away.

"I know I shouldn't have disturbed the crime scene," he whispered, "but I didn't want it to end up in the wrong hands." I nodded in agreement.

"I'm going to take her upstairs. She's not well," he said referring to Aprielle, who was in a state that I had never seen her in my thirty-something years in her employ. She didn't say one word, or even look my way. Her eyes were fixed forward, on something that apparently only she could see.

Rico took her upstairs and I immediately called Dr. Oatis. Although she was in excellent health for her age, I couldn't imagine what experiencing something so traumatic might have done to her. The fact that she hadn't said anything troubled me. She was always in complete control of everything around her, even under the most adverse circumstances, and she surely always had something to say.

When Dr. Oatis arrived, he examined her and assured Rico and me that she was fine. He said that she just needed to rest. He gave her a sedative to calm her nerves, and told us that it would probably have her out of it for a while.

After I saw Dr. Oatis out, I prepared Rico a cup of his favorite cocoa and some mint tea for myself. He was pretty shaken up, although he wasn't outwardly showing it.

I joined him in the study, where he had started a fire to combat the draft, and was relaxing on the couch. He recapped the story of the awful odor, Dr. Fitzgerald vomiting, Pebbles fainting, and the discovery of Maximillian and Paul's bodies. Pebbles sprawled out on the floor in one of her hooker outfits was more than I could have taken, but the thought of it gave me the comic relief I needed. We both laughed.

I picked the journal up from the table where I had placed it. It had once been a rich, chocolate brown with "MAX-IMILLIAN" in large capital letters prominently etched on its cover. The etching no longer had the depth and prominence it once had, and the color was now dull and faded from the years of handling. I had repeatedly tried to get him to let me send it back to the manufacturer so that they could restore it, a service they offered on their products. I had taken advantage of the service many times myself. They'd done a remarkable job of restoring my briefcases and purses to as good as new. He'd always refused. He said he liked it worn, because it reminded him of just how much his life had changed since the day Montgomery had given it to him and left for Europe.

I assured Rico that he had done the right thing by retrieving it. I put the journal back on the table. I really didn't want to think about it, or anything else. I really wanted someone to pinch me and wake me from what had to be a very bad dream.

I had been busy from the moment Rico had phoned me from the car with the news. First, trying to contact Camille and Dr. Klein in Delhi, and locate Mr. Hamilton who was on a safari in Africa. Then from the time Rico had returned with Aprielle, I'd been busy dealing with her and Dr. Oatis. I hadn't had time to even digest what was going on around me. It was nice to be able to just sit by the fire and sip my tea in silence.

The wind was blowing violently outside, rattling the shutters and swinging the trees to and fro. I slowly inhaled the tea's aroma—a failed attempt to clear my mind. I hoped that Camille and Dr. Klein would be able to get into the city okay. It was snowing so badly on the East Coast, that flights were being cancelled left and right. We were on storm watch ourselves. It was cold, dark and gloomy, very eerie under the circumstances and so unlike Maximillian. He had had a smile that could light the darkest day. I wanted so badly for him to walk into the room and bring me a little sunshine, like he'd done the day he peered into the world for the very first time.

Suddenly, my thoughts shifted to Paul and his family's loss. Paul was such a loving man, actually my favorite person at the

Center. He was always pleasant, and never too busy to see to the smallest detail. And the kids, they just loved him. They called him "Herringbone", which he got such a kick out of. Whenever one of the kids was in the hospital, he would, faithfully, go to visit them dressed as their favorite cartoon character.

I asked Rico if he knew if anyone had spoken to Paul's family. He didn't respond. I looked over at him. He'd fallen asleep, with his cup in hand. I took the cup, careful not to wake him, got a blanket from the closet and covered him. As I was putting the blanket over him, I was struck by the fact that he was as beautiful, after all these years, as the first day I'd seen him.

Chapter 2

It was the early sixties and due to complications with her pregnancy, Aprielle Hamilton was working temporarily from home, and needed an assistant. She had posted the position with the job placement center at the University of Detroit, where I was attending.

I submitted my resume, as did fifty other girls and a couple of boys. I was thrilled when I got the call that she wanted to see me. The first thing I did was called my girlfriend Diane, who had also applied for the position.

Diane was my friend and biggest rival. She was considered by most to be better looking than me and always went after—and got—everything I wanted, including head cheerleader and the star quarterback, William Buckram.

I had called Diane partly to tell her of my good news, but mostly to find out if she had gotten a call as well, and would be competition. She said that she hadn't heard anything, which made me ecstatic. I thanked God all the way to my car and even sent up a few extra prayers, to ensure that she wouldn't get one.

On the most important day of my life, my little Chevy would not start. I sat there, stroking the dash and pleading with her, "Come on, Pump, you can do it."

I called her Pump, because I had to pump the gas to get her to turn over. I didn't know if I had flooded her, or if the gas line was frozen, but I was pretty certain that those negative prayers I'd sent up against Diane were backfiring. Luckily, the university wasn't that far from where I had to go, so I decided to take the bus.

I boarded the Livernois bus to Seven Mile Road, then transferred to the eastbound bus on Seven Mile. When the bus started turning at Pontchartrain Boulevard, I panicked and ran to the front like a crazed lunatic. I had had no idea that the bus turned on Pontchartrain.

The driver told me that I was on the wrong bus. He said that I needed the East Seven Mile Road bus, which actually continued down Seven Mile Road. He gave me a transfer and showed me where to wait.

After about twenty minutes my feet were frozen and I was a nervous wreck. I knew that if I wanted the job, I absolutely could not be late. I had read that she was a real stickler about time.

I could see the exclusive neighborhood, through the naked trees in the distance. I realized that the house wasn't that far, so I decided to walk the rest of the way. Let me tell you, there is nothing worse than trekking through mountains of snow during high winds and bitter cold.

During my trek to the house I suddenly remembered, God rest her soul, one of my grandmother's silly little quips: *"All that looks like—Ain't!"* As country and silly as I had thought my grandmother's quips to be, that day that one had real meaning.

When I finally got to the house, I was completely out of breath and frozen half to death. I knocked on the door—traumatized, but on time.

Rico opened the door. The wind ripped inside, blowing snow into the foyer. He jumped behind the door, rubbing his massive arms with his equally massive hands. "Hurry, come in," he said. I quickly stepped in; that's when I got a good look at him. His beauty was captivating. Before that moment, I'd never thought of a man as beautiful.

I just stood there with my mouth hanging open and my eyes fixed on his. Handsome and cute absolutely and positively failed as descriptors. He had universal good looks. I suspected that he was mixed (that would be called bi-racial today). He was wearing sweats that clung to his large thighs, a Michigan State University tank top and no shoes. His body was smooth and well developed, and he had…well, an endowment he did nothing to conceal. I tried not to stare, but he caught me looking. He just smiled, extended his large hand and said, "Hello. I'm Rico. May I help you?"

A chill colder than the elements I had just endured rushed through my body. For a large man, his manner was gentle. I don't remember if I ever responded to his question, but I do remember him giving me some cocoa and going to get Aprielle, whom he referred to as "Mrs. H".

Chapter 3

"Good morning ma'am—tea?" This was my morning opener as I entered the study with a service for two. It had been nearly three months since I had answered the posting, accepted the job and came to work for Aprielle, the most admired and talked about woman in business.

"Good morning Gabrielle. Come in," she said, beckoning me with excitement, as if I were her best friend and she had a secret to share. I knew that was not the case. She didn't have any friends, at least none that I had met in my brief employ.

She was sitting at her desk, a very eminent piece of furniture, which gave the impression that the remainder of the room, done in pastels, had been created around it. Her accomplishments in the world of cosmetics dominated the room. Photographs covered with hand-written acknowledgments were everywhere. A photo of a woman and a little girl in an antique frame sat on the desk, a contrast to the rest of the room, which was very contemporary.

She had to be in her late thirties or early forties, which made her pregnancy a bit puzzling to me. Her age, like most everything about her, only she knew for sure. She was not beautiful or pretty. Aprielle's was a high-power sophisticated look, flawless and striking: the obvious result of her strong bone structure and experience with cosmetics. She wore Chanel almost exclusively. In her opinion, no one dressed a lady like Chanel. Her lean well-manicured hands were host to a 5-karat solitaire on her matrimony finger. She carefully sorted through a stack of photos, examining each one with prudence, as she jotted something onto her personalized writing pad.

"I'm having the most difficult time selecting appropriate second names for my little men," she said as I carefully poured the tea, noting the proper amount of lemon and honey for her cup.

"You've decided on a first?" I replied.

"Yes, the first born will be called Montgomery and the second, Maximillian," she said with complete confidence, as she did with all her decisions.

"What happened to Shawn and Corey, Mr. Hamilton seemed so fond of those names?"

"Shawn and Corey," she repeated, clearly to reinforce that I had just insulted her.

"Shawns and Coreys are not individuals you take seriously, Gabrielle. A name can make all the difference in the world. This is why I insist that you do not allow people to address you as Gabby. It creates an utterly immature image of you." I wished I hadn't asked. "I am about to give birth to two of the world's most powerful men, and I will not make the mistake of giving them names inappropriate for their station," she continued, rubbing her stomach like a queen carrying the heir apparent. "My difficulty is in selecting a second name strong enough to follow the first."

"What if they're girls?" As I asked the question, I realized its inaptness, but it was too late.

"Gabrielle, I have the best obstetrician in the country," she said. Of course she knew what sex they were. She launched into her self-made woman speech, the one that anyone who had spent more than fifteen minutes with her had heard. For most it was interesting, others entertaining, but for those who had heard it over and over, it left them feeling like it was nothing more than her personal ego bath. I had heard it so many times that I could actually recite it word for word. I had quickly figured out, however, that it wasn't about her ego at all. It was just her way of reminding herself that all this was real. It was about her fear that one day she'd wake up from this dream she was living.

She had created an empire. As president, CEO, and major stockholder of Hamilton International, the world's leading cosmetic company, she had accomplished something that most women couldn't fathom and most men found hard to accept. Out of sheer admiration and respect, for the one thousand, three hundred and twenty-sixth time I listened, occasionally lip syncing along with her, when I was sure she couldn't see me.

When she finished, I expected us to move on like we always did after what I called a *lesson a la Aprielle*. She had this way of indirectly teaching me little lessons through her tirades. Instead of moving on she picked up the antique framed photo from her desk, the one she'd never spoken about.

I assumed it was she and her mother, but that had never been confirmed. "This woman knew so little pleasure," she said referring to the woman in the photo, "she sold her soul to the man who broke her, working herself to death cooking and cleaning his home and the homes of white women. His role as the quote, unquote man was to punish her when she had an opinion other than his, even about the money that she earned, and he drank up. She secretly took in ironing on weekends, while he was away on his sex and alcohol binges, to earn enough for me to go to private school, a waste in his opinion. She decided that where I went to school would be our business. He never knew. She insisted that I learn not only the books but also another way of life. At Our Lady of Mercy I watched my well-bred classmates driven to school in big black cars, dressed in the finest apparel money could buy. I moved through those corridors with an air and posture, if in no other way equal, equally as privileged in knowing that this was also my world, although it took me two hours and three buses to get there. She would always say, 'April Louise, honey, leave assumptions to the lazy and the hopeful. Never assume that the world owes you anything or that men folk gone give ya anything. Know that with faith, hard work and the grace of God, you can have anything your heart desires.' I never forgot that."

"She was a very wise woman," I said, shocked at how revealing she was being. Up until that moment she had not revealed anything to me about her past.

In order to appear knowledgeable about her and her company, before my original interview I read her biography, which opened with a very interesting quote: "The past is experiences had, nothing more, nothing less, and dwelling on it is at best, a waste of the present." I'd found her to be an incredibly fascinating woman who had made some very calculated and profitable choices in her life. Regrettably, the biography focused solely on her rise to the top of the world of cosmetics and said nothing about her upbringing. Greta, the kitchen staff supervisor, had told me that her mom had passed away a few years before I came to work for her and that no one knew anything about her father.

She returned the picture to her desk. I was silent. The energy in the room had changed. I had already become accustomed to her changing a room's energy, but this was very uncomfortable. I tried to lighten the mood, "I'm convinced that if she were here, ma'am, she'd tell you that you are way too far along in your pregnancy to be wearing those pumps!"

"Have the new packaging designs arrived?" she asked, changing the subject like she often did to express her disapproval or depleted interest in the conversation.

"I spoke to Randy—"

"Randal," she interrupted.

I'm sorry, I meant Randal. I spoke with him and asked him to send us—"

"Gabrielle," she interrupted again, "you don't *ask* Randal to send me anything, you *tell* him! Get him on the line."

She had become agitated. She became agitated over the simplest things. It was hard to understand her. It seemed I always either said too much, too little, or the inappropriate. Sometimes she made me feel like a child, and inside I was desperately praying for the day that her newborns would be taking that place. Of course, I didn't move fast enough, so she dialed Randy herself using the speakerphone.

It fascinated me how she balanced rather gracefully between a powerful ball-breaking bitch and an angel. As she relaxed back into her chair I caught a glimpse of the angel. I decided I'd better watch carefully, this was probably going to be a *lesson a la Aprielle.*

"Good morning, Hamilton International. Lisa speaking. How may I help you?"

"Randal Shelby, please."

"I'm sorry, Mr. Shelby is in a meeting, would you like to leave a message?"

"Tell him that Aprielle Hamilton is on the line." She didn't like it when staff didn't recognize her voice. She considered them unobservant and a detriment to the company.

"Whom?"

"Whom? Did you say whom, young lady?"

"Yes, ma'am." Although she was managing to remain polite, I could tell by her voice that she was becoming impatient with Aprielle.

"First of all, Lisa, it's who. You did say Lisa?"

"Yes!"

"Secondly, I would like to test your observation. Have you ever noticed whose signature appears on your check?"

"No ma'am, I can't say that I have."

"Fine, tomorrow when you receive your check, note whose signature appears and you will understand why it is your final one. Now tell Randal that Mrs. Hamilton is tired of waiting." Poor Lisa, she didn't say anything. She just put the call through.

Randy was one of the drabbest looking, most boring men I had ever met. I don't know what women saw in him. He was a little on the chubby side and wore these 1950's black horn-rim glasses. He let his hair grow out on one side, so he could comb it over the top of his bald spot. He was hideous, but he always managed to have a very attractive woman on his arm.

As Hamilton International's lead packaging designer, he had a lot of clout with the company. Aprielle felt that the product's packaging was as important as, if not more important than, the content. She had lured him away from her competitor about five years prior. He loved working for her, although she was extremely tough on him and his team. He picked up.

"Aprielle, darling, calling to inform me that you've given birth to my replacement? Huh, huh!" He laughed, with that ridiculous laugh that made you want to bop him over the head with one of those rubber chickens. He had about as much personality as a doorknob.

"Mr. Shelby, I do not need that. What I do need, however, is the MX-17 packaging designs—today! They aren't complete? You ran into a few problems? You just forwarded me a report detailing the situation, with some sample mock-ups?" She repeated each excuse as he delivered it.

"Randal Shelby, I do not want mock-ups. I want this line launched on schedule, and the way I see it, you are holding it up. I want you, Jerry, and Angela in my office first thing tomorrow morning with a complete presentation."

"Come to Detroit?" he asked.

"I am certainly not coming to New York. Advise Personnel to replace Ms. Lisa, the operator. There is no room at this company for individuals who are lazy and unobservant. It is in that position that you take the opportunity to learn the company, our clients, our products and prepare to move forward, not snack, paint your nails, and wait for the phone to ring. If there is a problem with any of you making it tomorrow morning, 9 a.m. sharp, do not bother to call me with excuses, simply retrieve your final checks with Lisa. Good day!" Without waiting for a response, she disengaged the call and summoned the morning mail. So much for the angel, I thought.

Rico entered with an armful of envelopes. I rose to get them. She motioned for me to remain seated. "Here, make yourself useful," she said and handed me the photos. I sorted through them as she went through the mail.

I couldn't stop thinking about Rico, whose scent was still in the room. Like clockwork each morning at dawn, he concluded his workout with laps in the Hamilton pool.

I'd watched him from my window. He'd position himself on the high board, his entry always magic. The water seemed to welcome him to their daily dance ritual of motion and resistance, fully cooperating with his every move. When the dance was done he would propel himself from the pool, gently breaking their embrace…his liquid partner finding its way down the muscular pathway of his back, patiently awaiting the next day's dawn. Although neither he nor Mrs. Hamilton had ever given any indication, I had a feeling that he was sleeping with her. It was in those moments that I indeed wanted to be her.

She started ripping up the documents and barking about them being rehashed concepts. Suddenly she was overcome by something more powerful than she was. She let out a wail and doubled over, calling my name. I rushed over to her. "Listen carefully," she said, "My water has broken. Alert Dr. Oatis, have Rico bring the car around—my bag is in the hall closet—redirect tomorrow's meeting to the hospital. Hurry along Gabrielle, these boys are not willing to wait!"

Chapter 4

It was a difficult labor. When we got to the hospital, her contractions were twenty minutes apart. I kept trying to reach Mr. Hamilton, who was at a convention in Seattle. He was so thrilled about becoming a father that he had considered not going to Seattle, but Aprielle had insisted. Since she wasn't due for another two weeks, he'd thought that he would get back in plenty of time. I kept trying to reach him.

I finally reached him around eight o'clock. Before I could finish my sentence, I heard a dial tone on the other end of the line. I thought that maybe he had fainted when he heard me say "labor". I called him right back—he answered. "Are you okay?" I asked.

"I'm fine!" he said, obviously thrilled by the news. "I'll be on the next flight. I think there's one that leaves here around 11:55. Tell her to hold on, I'm coming."

In his excitement, he'd hung up again before I could warn him that she wasn't in the best of moods. She'd been driving the nursing staff mad with her demands, and she'd been cursing him from the moment we'd arrived at the hospital. I told Rico that I thought that he should meet Mr. H at the airport, so that he didn't kill himself trying to get there. With that taken care of, I returned to Aprielle's bedside.

Maximillian was born at 11:46 p.m. Montgomery, apparently on his own timetable, arrived twenty-seven minutes later—feet first. This scared the stew out of me. I knew how dangerous breach births could be, but Montgomery stepped in without complication, like he owned the world.

Because of Montgomery's delayed arrival, the boys didn't share the same birth date. This always had to be explained; for some reason people, had a problem comprehending that one twin was born before midnight and the other one after. I really didn't think it was that complicated.

I was on my way to the cafeteria when I spotted Mr. Hamilton gazing into the nursery. He was so engrossed in watching the boys that he didn't see me come up behind him, "Mr. H, how long have you been here?"

"I just arrived. They told me downstairs that they had already been delivered, so I came straight here. How's Aprielle?"

"She's sleeping."

"Look at them, Gabby, aren't they beautiful?"

They were adorable, with the same big brown eyes and unbelievably long lashes, which was a clear indicator to me that they were destined to be handsome, in an indisputable way. They had a head full of hair that trailed slightly down the sides of their little faces. If it weren't for their identification tags, we couldn't have known them apart. They weighed 4lbs., 6 oz. each and were 15″ in length. The doctor said that as they got bigger they would probably develop some physical distinctions, but if not, their personalities, or childhood injuries would definitely distinguish them.

It was clear from the very beginning, that although they looked exactly alike, they were as different as night and day. Maximillian lay quietly, while Montgomery kicked and waved his little arms all over the place.

The naming order somehow got mixed up, with Maximillian being given to the first born, and Montgomery to the second. This was a hospital error. Well, we were never really sure if it was the hospital or Mr. Hamilton who mixed up the naming order, but one thing was certain, Aprielle was beside herself with fury. She filed a lawsuit against the hospital, naming everyone in the delivery room and anyone associated with the births as defendants.

Randy and his staff called to congratulate her and offer their regrets for not being able to be there. A snowstorm had them grounded in Chicago. She fired them. Later that day, following her meeting with Tyler, her psychic advisor, she dropped the lawsuit and rehired the design team. Tyler assured her that the name mix up and the snowstorm were positive omens; besides, she wanted to be very careful about the kind of energy that she projected, particularly in the first few months, because her actions could bring negative vibrations to the boys.

After giving Aprielle her personal forecast, Tyler charted individual forecasts for each of the boys. Generally speaking, in astrology, when you are born on what is called the cusp, at the end of one sign and the beginning of the next, you tend to have the traits of both. Tyler explained that that was an over-generalization at best and when charted properly your true nature and influences could be revealed.

Although the majority of their planets were in the same houses, Maximillian was definitely Cardinal-Earth Capricorn, the highest embodiment of the practical power to deal with the material world. He was destined to succeed in life because of his combined thoroughness and ambition, and that his Saturn rulership would make him very conscious of time and the principles of restraint. Tyler cautioned Aprielle that Maximillian would tend to repress his emotions and inspirations, focusing them into his work. He would, however, be very passionate, but would hold his passion in check, waiting for the right opportunity to lavish his love on one all-consuming desire. In fact, his path to ultimate success would probably be through denial.

Montgomery, on the other hand, was Fixed-Air Aquarius, ruled by the eccentric power of Uranus, endowing him with the optimism and belief that problems would solve themselves in unexpected and unconventional ways, if you just let events take their course. He'd seem cool or detached because of his tendency to shy away from emotional involvement; particularly those that threaten to restrict his mental freedom. He would be dedicated to the exploration of ideas as abstract concepts. Aprielle was cautioned that Montgomery would definitely be a classic nonconformist, thoroughly modern and open to all kinds of ideas, always picking and choosing those that best fit his vision of his future.

Aprielle was both pleased and concerned. Maximillian's conservative and cautious qualities, coupled with her guidance, seemed a perfect formula for success, but Montgomery's experimental, nonconformist ways sounded like a predisposition for trouble. She was an Aries and could certainly appreciate a sense of adventure, but she also knew many Aquarians and had witnessed first hand the complexities of their superior intellect and their obsession with freedom, which so often kept too many of them on endless roads to nowhere. Aprielle was certain that Montgomery was going to be more than a handful. Tyler told her that Mr. H, a Leo, would be better suited to deal with Montgomery, since Leo and Aquarius are opposites on the wheel of life and tend to respect one another.

Aprielle was confident that the boys would be fine. She was just glad to have the whole thing behind her, so that she could get back to New York and her work full time.

Chapter 5

The phones had been ringing off the hook all morning with reporters calling, trying to confirm the deaths of Dr. Hamilton and Paul Harrell. "There must be some mistake," I said, "Dr. Hamilton and Mr. Harrell are in Delhi at a wellness conference." I kept that line up until I saw the morning paper.

> Dr. Maximillian Hamilton, renowned pediatrician, founder of the Riverfront Wellness Complex, heir to the Hamilton cosmetic empire and brother of openly gay talk show personality Montgomery Hamilton-Ross was found dead in his office with his assistant, Paul Harrell. It appears to be a love affair gone bad, murder-suicide. According to Detroit police the case is still under investigation, and they have not ruled out foul play. Dr. Hamilton was most widely known for his pioneering work in transforming America's healthcare

*delivery system, from that of treating symptoms of
disease as the primary thrust to a health mainte-
nance model…*

What in the world! Why would a reputable newspaper
print such a story without corroborating it? I immediately
called Richard Hackney, the family attorney. "Richard, this
is Gabby. Have you seen the morning paper?"

"No, I haven't," he said still groggy, having been awakened
by my call.

"You'd better read it. Max's murder is on the front page
and those leeches are saying that it's a love affair gone bad
murder-suicide. After all he's done for this community, how
could they do this to him?"

"They're just trying to sell papers, Gabby. Don't worry. I'll
handle it." He hoped that the paper had taken a chance at an
exclusive by running the story, and that it wasn't officially on
the wire yet.

"I'll tell them that the story is completely untrue and
threaten litigation. Don't you worry your pretty little head
about it. When this has all blown over, will you let me take
you to dinner?"

"Richard Hackney, how many times do I have to tell
you, no?"

"I guess until you say yes," he replied.

"Goodbye, Richard!" I said hanging up the phone. I was
definitely attracted to him and loved the way he said my
name, with that deep bravado of his, but I couldn't go out
with him. As a rule I don't date men that do business with

Aprielle, or who are in her employ, which unfortunately for me, rules out just about every man I come in contact with.

I turned on the television. The media frenzy had begun. It was all over the news. I flipped through the channels. It was the top story on every station. Aprielle had discussed the delicate nature of the situation with both the Chief of Police and the Coroner, who were her friends. They agreed to handle things discretely. She knew that did not really amount to very much, since money-hungry cops and clerks at the coroner's office routinely leaked information to the press. She'd hoped to buy enough time for her people to develop an appropriate spin. This whole thing could end up costing Hamilton International a small fortune.

I finished reading the article to get an idea of what was out there. The story continued on three pages. I was shocked at how much accurate information they actually had about the family. I prayed that Montgomery had not seen any of this. It was still early on the West Coast, so there was a good chance he hadn't. Lord knows I didn't want him finding out about the sudden and gruesome death of his brother from some insensitive reporter.

I debated whether or not to call him now and wake him, or wait. He got up round 5:30 for his workout. I checked the time. It was 6:18 our time. I still had a couple of hours. I decided to deal with things on this side of the country first. I showed Aprielle the paper and told her about the news reports. I wanted her to know that the cat was out of the bag, so to speak. She wasn't herself and understandably so. She had come up against many things in her days, but none had prepared her for the loss of Maximillian. When I entered the room I could see the sedative still had her pretty much out of it.

"Gabrielle, is that you honey?"

"Yes, it's me." She tried to get up.

"You don't have to get up," I said.

"But I need to make…"

"You don't need to do anything but rest," I told her and helped her back into the bed. I propped the pillows up behind her. "I called Wendy and suggested that she close the office for a few days, and I talked to Jerry and gave him an update. I also called Hackney. He's formalizing a strategy and will get back to us," I said.

"A strategy, what strategy? At this point it is simply about damage control. Richard is just trying to put some more of my money in his pocket. That man is so shamelessly corrupt, it isn't funny. That is why I have him on my team," she laughed.

"You should probably call down to The Center and tell what's-her-name."

"Pebbles," I said.

"I'm sorry, I just cannot bring myself to call a grown woman Pebbles. If that is not the most ridiculous name I have ever heard, I do not know what is. Anyway, give her Jerry's number and tell her not to make any statements— none! Tell her Camille and Dr. Klein will handle things when they get back."

"By the way," I said, "I managed to track down the safari coordinator, they're going to get a message to Mr. Hamilton right away."

"Thank you, Gabrielle. You are so effective that I cannot imagine what I would do without you. I told that man before he left here to take his cell phone with him, but does he listen to me? No! He claimed taking a phone defeated the purpose. Now, if we were to leave his smart behind out there, then he would understand my point. That is the purpose of having a cell phone in the first place."

"You know he has his own way," I replied.

"One that, obviously, only he understands. I cannot figure out, to save my life, why anybody in his right mind would want to spend two weeks in the jungle, anyway," she said, shaking her head.

She could be sweet when she wanted to be. Mr. H was probably the perfect man for a woman like her, easygoing, but certainly not a pushover. I think the sedative had her so relaxed that she couldn't have been mean if she had wanted to be.

As I got up to leave the room, I thought, now is as good a time as any. I paused, took a deep breath and said, "I was going to call Montgomery to tell him what happened before the media does, but I really think that it would be better if it came from you, particularly under the circumstances." She didn't respond. She had had very little to say to or about Montgomery after he had ditched law school and run off to Europe…a stunt she thought to be selfish and childish.

She'd finally written him off completely after he threatened her with a custody battle over his daughter Jade, whom she had taken care of from birth. Mr. H eventually had had to intervene and convince her that it was best to just let Jade go.

"You can call him or let him find out from the media. Either way he will be informed. That is the point, is it not?" she said.

"You are dead wrong," I snapped. "That boy has just lost the most important person in the world to him, and you are suggesting that his finding out from the media is an option that gets to the point. That is your son and the only one you have left, do I need to remind you?"

"Do not use that tone with me. If he was that damn important to him, he would have never run off to Europe and left him. Montgomery is my son, but he had no respect for me or this family, and son or not, I will not tolerate it."

"We both know why he did that. You weren't exactly…" I stopped myself. My voice had elevated several octaves and I indeed wanted to slap some sense into her, but I knew it was not the time for a fight I couldn't win. I turned and quickly left the room without another word. I headed for my office to handle the calls.

"Get out! You're fired!" She yelled down the hall at me. "I want you off these premises immediately…Ricooooo!" she screamed. I just shook my head. She had fired me so many times over the years, neither one of us could keep count, nor bothered to. I passed Rico in the hall.

"What's going on?" he asked.

"Ricoooooooooo!" she continued screaming.

"She's just being her cantankerous old self," I said. He smiled, and headed towards her room as I headed to my office.

Chapter 6

As I sat down to make the calls, I was reminded of how glad I was that Aprielle had decided to move the executive offices to Detroit, leaving production, distribution, and research and development in New York. She still kept an apartment in Manhattan, but unless there was a particular launch party or special event she needed to attend, we rarely went to New York anymore.

Right after the boys were born, Aprielle had been anxious to get back to New York to make sure things hadn't started to slip in her absence. Initially, we, including the boys and their nanny, were commuting back and forth, spending the weekdays in New York and the weekends here. Eventually, we were spending the majority of our time in New York, not returning for weeks at a time, which really bothered Mr. H, because he rarely got to see the boys.

This went on until the boys became school-aged. Mr. H had thought it best that the boys attend school in Michigan.

When Aprielle was finally convinced that she could run things comfortably from here and the boys turned five, she moved the headquarters to Troy, a suburb just north of here.

The plan had been to work from the house until the Troy offices were renovated, however, after their completion, we continued to conduct business from the house. I don't think I can say that I've been to the Troy offices more than five or six times in thirty years.

The greatest thing about our move to Michigan, besides reducing the amount of travel, was that it successfully insulated me from the company politics. This side of the cosmetic business is anything but glamorous. I suppose wherever there is lots of money to be made, you can count on there being backstabbing and conniving, and this industry is no different.

Immediately following the move back here, she asked me to consider moving into the four-room suite situated on the upper back corner of the house. At first I was a little apprehensive, but I realized that my responsibilities kept me with her almost twenty-four hours a day, so I did. The space was much better than my little apartment, with a bedroom, a sitting room, an office/library, and a wet room, complete with sauna, steam room, and a full set of workout equipment. After I moved in, I actually found time to sit in the Jacuzzi and relax every once in a while.

Shortly after I settled in, she asked me to schedule an appointment with Jacqueline, her decorator. I was under the impression that she was going to redo her office, which she did every few years.

At the last minute, she asked me to take the meeting, due to a scheduling conflict. That sort of tipped me off. I handle all of her appointments, and in all my years with her there had only been one scheduling conflict and I made sure that never happened again.

During a pre-holiday season rush, I accidentally scheduled two very important meetings on the same day, at the same time—my first mistake. Both meetings required her attendance, which of course was impossible. When I realized the blunder, I quickly tried to reschedule one of the meetings, but couldn't get another appointment until after the guy returned from the holidays. This resulted in the company losing revenue—my second mistake.

She gave me two choices: empty my desk and vacate the premises or repay the loss. I chose to repay the loss. She had Accounting calculate the exact amount and deduct it from my pay over a two-year period. On the day of the final deduction she called me into her office.

"Do you know what today is?" she asked.

"Wednesday," I said, puzzled.

"It is the anniversary of your little scheduling blunder."

"Oh, that," I was not amused. That blunder, as she called it, had cost me dearly.

"Here is a little something to show my appreciation for your honor and loyalty," she said. She handed me an envelope. I opened it. Inside, there was a check and a letter that read:

Gabrielle,

It is rare that you encounter people with true character, especially in this business. I must say that I was truly surprised when you took the option of repaying the lost revenues that resulted from your scheduling mistake. I thought that you would empty your desk and that would be the last time I saw you. Even after you agreed to repay the money, I thought that eventually you would become bitter and quit. That was not the case, you took responsibility for your mistake, repaid every penny, and remained a superior employee in the process, never coming to me once to complain or try to renegotiate the situation, which I would have done.

For your commitment, loyalty, and superior service, enclosed you will find a bonus check and documentation of your 25% pay increase, effective immediately. Thank you for your loyalty.

Her gesture knocked the water right out of my eyes. By the time I had finished the letter I was a mess. When I saw the check I thought I was going to come completely unglued. It was three times the amount I had repaid.

I took the meeting with Jacqueline, as requested. When I arrived, Aprielle was sitting there, chatting and having tea. Come to find out, the meeting was actually a surprise for me to pick out fabrics and discuss with Jacqueline how I wanted my new space decorated. She could be a very generous woman when she wanted to be.

Chapter 7

The calls were taking longer than I had expected. Of course, everyone had a million questions, most of which neither the police nor I could answer at this point. It was already eight o'clock our time. I decided I'd better try Monte. "Disconnected!" I must have misdialed, an indicator to me that I really didn't want to be the bearer of this news. I wished she would quit being so stubborn and make amends with him, especially now that he was all she had left. I tried to call again. The machine picked up: "*No one is available right now. Please leave your message after the tone.*" That's strange, I thought. Where's Artier? He always answered the phone at the house. I hate it when people use those silly computer greetings; you never know if you have the right number or not. I took a chance and left a message. "Monte, Zoren, I hope I have the right number. This is Gabby. Call me as soon as you get this message. It's very important." I decided to also leave a message at the studio just in case.

I hated calling the studio, I actually felt funny when I called there. Now that Montgomery's a big television personality, there are all these people around him whose job is to prevent him from being accessed. It's not like I ever had a problem getting a message to him, and he always called me back right away, but it still felt strange. Sometimes I wanted to say, "For God's sake, I changed his darn diapers, just put him on the phone," but I understand it's just part of the life he lives. It must be hard not to be able to go places without being bothered by people. I guess that's what you give up when you choose to live in the public eye.

Surprisingly, Montgomery's fame caused minimal problems for the family. It affected Maximillian more than anyone; from time to time people mistook him for Montgomery. That usually only happened when he was out of town. Most people locally knew Maximillian very well, and didn't confuse him with Montgomery.

About ten years ago Montgomery signed a big domestic television deal for his show *Hamilton-Ross*, which had been a huge success in the UK. The show premiered here in the fall of '91 and took off like a rocket. The show's success has been attributed to Montgomery's raw style, wit, and ability to say the things most people think, but are afraid to say.

It's remained among the top rated shows on television since its premiere. Thanks to the success of *Hamilton-Ross* and two other prime-time hits that they write and produce, Monte and his partner and co-host, Zoren Ross, have been unofficially dubbed the biggest TV duo since Desi and Lucy.

The fact that they're men hasn't seemed to matter, probably because most Americans think of them as foreigners. Rico and I both watch their show whenever we can, unlike Aprielle, who has never seen it. I tape it and clip all the articles about them for her in case one day she comes around. So far she hasn't.

I decided to try Jade's line.

Chapter 8

I was just about to dial Jade's number when I heard Camille coming in. She came directly into the office where I was, poured herself a scotch and lit a cigarette. She looked weary. "Honey, you look exhausted." I said.

Her clothes were rumpled and she was in desperate need of a touch-up, which surprised me because Camille never let her hair go.

"Girl, I am," she said. "They had us sitting on that damn runway at JFK for five hours."

"Five hours?" I inquired. Camille had a tendency to exaggerate. So I often repeated her statements back to her. It was my way of giving her an opportunity to retract some of the ridiculous things she said.

"Five fuckin' hours, do you hear me? De-icing the wings, and changing their damn minds back and forth about whether they were going to take off at all."

"I've been listening to the advisories all morning. I was afraid that you might get grounded in New York."

"I wish we had been officially grounded; at least we could have gotten off that hot-ass plane. I felt sorry for them poor folks cramped up back in coach. Shit, I couldn't 'ave done it." Another example: prior to marrying Maximillian, coach was all she knew, but somehow she'd forgotten that. I chose not to challenge it. "How's Dr. Klein?" I asked.

"He's a whole other story. I'll get to that, but first I've got to tell you about those incompetent asses at the airline. Because of all the cancellations and delays and shit, we ended up flying through Chicago. When we got to Chicago all of the flights to Detroit were booked. I figured, we're First Class passengers, so of course we'd be getting a little priority. Well, I just happened to overhear the reservationist upgrading this white bitch to first class on the same flight the bitch had told me there were no more seats. Gabby, you know I straight clowned!"

"You didn't," I said, knowing full well that she did. She relished in the opportunity to 'get somebody told' as she put it.

"Mind you, we had sat on the runway in New York for so long, I had to have drunk the bar dry, so by the time we got to Chicago, I had a nice buzz on."

"What did you do?" I asked, not sure I really wanted to know.

"Let's just say, I had to put that Dr. Ellis, Harvard educated bullshit aside and go straight to Baltimore on that bitch. I told her, 'Look, I am not the bitch to be fucked with, not today, not any day. I've 'bout had it up to here with planes, airports and everything associated with this motherfucker, so before you go upgrading anybody to anything, I suggest you find me, that's Dr. Ellis (E-L-L-I-S), and my traveling companion Dr. Klein, seats on the next thing out of here. Are you feelin' me?' Oh, girl she tells me that she's already gotten Klein a seat. Why'd she tell me that shit? Now you know what that was about. Before I knew it, I had collared that bitch up and security was pullin' my black ass up off of her.

"Klein, Mr. Diplomat himself, explained everything and told 'em that I was understandably under a lot of stress and not myself due to Max's sudden death. They let us go without incident and immediately boarded us. I know they wanted to straight get rid of my crazy ass.

"Once we got settled on the flight, Klein's ass gon' try to reprimand me—please! Talkin' about, I embarrassed him and the Center. Like I give a fuck about embarrassing him. Jews kill me, they the first ones crying foul, if they so much as think whitey is tryin' to pull some anti-Semitic shit, but then he gon' trip with me, when it was obvious that that ho was trying to give me the nigger treatment. Fuck him!"

She laughed to herself and poured another drink. I watched as she poured what looked like a triple, and thought how as much as some things change, others stayed the same.

When Camille had married Maximillian she didn't drink. She had been adamant that she'd take a joint over a drink any day. "Alcohol makes you stupid," she'd said. Based on what she had just described, she had been right.

When Aprielle had discovered that Camille smoked marijuana, she'd had a closed door meeting with Maximillian about the matter. She'd insisted that he put a stop to it immediately. She'd even suggested that if Camille absolutely needed something to relax, escape, or whatever she had been trying to accomplish with marijuana, she should try something socially acceptable—like brandy.

Camille had had a particularly difficult time adjusting to the responsibilities that came with marrying into the family and Aprielle had done nothing to make it easier for her. She had frequently met with Maximillian to discuss Camille and what she'd referred to as her "ghetto ways". She had tried to be civil with Camille for Maximillian's sake, but her feelings had been clear—Camille had not been her choice. As a matter of fact, she'd felt that Maximillian had scraped the bottom of the barrel when he'd married her.

Camille had grown up in a poor, drug-torn area of Baltimore, the youngest of four children. Her brothers had all but raised her. Jeremy, her brother closest to her, had kept after her about her studies, so that she wouldn't end up pregnant too soon like their mother had, in jail like their two older brothers, or living perilously like him on the street selling drugs. His strict guidance and her natural intellect had won her a scholarship to Harvard, where she'd met

Maximillian. I had been convinced that Aprielle hated Camille so much, because she reminded her of her own painful, poverty-filled past.

"Camille, was all that necessary?" I asked.

"I'm here ain't I?"

"Camille, it's not what you do. It's…"

"Don't give me that bullshit. It's about the outcome. Once I dropped all that polite articulate shit she got me a seat like she should have done in the first damn place. Anyway, enough about that, where's the crabby old woman?" she said, referring to Aprielle.

"She's upstairs resting. Dr. Oatis gave her a sedative."

"Sedative! Aprielle sedated. Shit, it must be my lucky day. Speaking of sedatives. I didn't realize Klein talked so damn much. He talked the entire nine hours from Delhi to London, and for another six hours and fifty minutes from London to New York. About midway between Heathrow and JFK, I was looking in my purse trying to find something to put his talkin' ass to sleep. I even asked the flight attendant if she had anything we could slip into his juice. She just smiled. She just didn't know. I was serious as hell."

"Camille, you know darn well that they can't give you as much as an aspirin on an airplane," I said.

"I wasn't thinking. I just wanted to shut his talkin'-ass up. Finally, I just had to say, 'would you pa-lease shut the fuck up!'"

"Now, that wasn't nice."

"Why are you defending him?" she said.

"I'm not defending anybody. You know that wasn't nice."

"He'll get over it. He's such a little wimp. I can barely stand him. He's all worried about the future of the Center. He knows Fitzgerald isn't committed. He's afraid things will fall apart with Max gone."

"He's got a point," I said.

"I don't plan to be around there to find out."

"What do you mean?"

"You'll see. Max *would* wait 'til we get all the way to Delhi to kill his fool-self."

"Camille!" I figured it must be the stress talking.

"What?"

"Why would you say something like that?"

"Like what? Shit, Max knows how I am about flying. I wasn't thrilled that he agreed to have that damn conference in Delhi in the first place, but he insisted, arguing that the West needed to reach out more. So I spend nineteen hours flying halfway across the globe, in the spirit of reaching out, only to have to turn right around and spend another nineteen hours in the air and five on a runway, because the man who put this whole thing together decides to kill his-fool-self. That shit's crazy. He's about nuttier than his momma."

"I can't sit here and listen to you carry on like this. I know this is hard for you, but you have got to pull yourself together."

"I'm fine! Quiet as it's kept, he just saved me a whole lot of trouble. I was divorcing his ass when I got back anyway. I knew he was fuckin' that boy."

"What are you talking about?"

"Like you didn't know."

"Know what?"

"That Maximillian was fuckin' Paul Harrell"

"You don't actually believe that?"

"Um hum."

"He loved you."

"And?"

"And that meant something to him, you know that."

"Whatever."

"He and Paul were associates."

"You're worse than his damn momma. I lived with Maximillian for fifteen years and he was so disconnected from himself, I don't think he knew what he felt. He might have had y'all fooled with all that Mr. Perfect, all around family and community man shit, not me. Remember that I'm the one with the Doctorate in Psychiatry, and I conclude that the only difference between he and Montgomery was integrity—something, I must say, I've always admired about Montgomery. Don't get me wrong, I don't believe he was acting on his feelings until recently. He certainly wasn't fuckin' me. When I confronted him about it, he denied it. I told him to replace Paul, because anybody in his right mind could see that Paul wanted him. He refused. Keeping Paul was apparently more important than keeping his wife. You figure it out."

"I don't believe it. You and the media are speculating and rushing to judgement."

"I'm ain't judging shit. There ain't shit to judge—to each his own! I'm merely sharing my observation. It seems to me that the newspapers got more sense than you do. Two half–naked, grown-ass men are found dead together, and one of them is holding a gun. I mean, do I need to paint you a picture? That's about as above suspicion as Michael Jackson's tired, old, rusty ass having sleepovers with ten year olds."

I was horrified by what she was saying. Camille could be uncouth and tacky, but this was a bit much, even for her.

"You're wrong," I told her. "He was your husband and the father of your children."

"And?"

"And he loved you!"

"I believe that too. As much as he could love anybody."

"Then how can you say these things?"

"I'm not saying anything wrong by pointing out the truth. If you don't think I'm telling the truth, that's one thing. But if you think it's bad or shameful that the truth is that he was probably gay too, then you need to reexamine some things, particularly the sincerity of your feelings toward Montgomery, who happens to be gay in case you forgot. Max was a good man, who took great care of his children and other folks as well, which is more than most men are willing to do. The enormous contributions Maximillian made to this family and the medical community does not erase his confusion and lack of sense of self. Gabby, Max was a very unhappy man."

Max's journal immediately came to mind. "Rico brought Max's journal from the office. It's in the study. I'll get it for you. I didn't read it," I said. I got up to go and get it so I could give it to her.

"Why not?" she replied.

"I didn't think it was appropriate."

"He's dead. He certainly won't care!"

"Why are you being so insensitive? I just thought you might…"

"Might what?" she interrupted. "Want his journal? I don't need Max's journal to tell me what I already know. You keep it! I strongly suggest that you read it too, since you can't pull your head out of his mother's ass long enough to see the obvious. I'll bet you everything I've got that the man in those pages is not the man you thought you knew. I'm very sorry that you find my comments insensitive." She started gathering up her things. "I thought it was candid conversation among family. I hate to abruptly end our little visit, but I need to get home." She buzzed Greta on the intercom.

"Greta, hi it's Camille, would you please get Max and Madison ready to go."

"They're finishing their breakfast, Ms. Camille. I'll get them cleaned up as soon as they're done." The children apparently heard their mother's voice; we could hear them in the background screaming. "It's Mommy, Mommy's home." Before she could get off with Greta, the kids were in the office jumping all over Camille.

"Mommy, Mommy!"

"How are my little rug rats? Did you two miss Mommy?" she said.

"Yeah!" they screamed in unison.

"Go and let Greta wipe your faces and put your coats on. Give Aunt Gabby a kiss bye-bye."

"Bye, Aunt Gabby." They hugged and kissed me.

"Why don't you let Rico drive you home?" I suggested.

"Max's car is out front. I'll be fine." I motioned toward her empty scotch glass, so I wouldn't have to come right out and say she'd had quite a bit to drink in front of the children. She sighed, rolled her eyes, and reluctantly said, "Call Rico."

Rico told me to tell her to meet him out front. Camille's account had me ill at ease. It was as if she was talking about a completely different person. I went into the study to get the journal. Was she right? I wanted to know. I sat down and opened it.

November 17, 1997
Paul informed me that the research grant is in. He invited me to go out with him again. I told him…

I shut it and pulled it tight to my bosom and contemplated whether I should read any further. I felt like reading it would be a violation of some sort. I was holding what amounted to his most private intimate thoughts. Maybe Camille was wrong about him caring if others read them, and maybe she was wrong about him. All I knew for sure was that he had shown me the man he wanted me to know. A wonderful human being that had never been anything but kind and generous to me. Maybe I should just leave it at that. Besides, I still needed to call Montgomery. Then it hit me, one of my grandmother's quips: *"Just 'cause it walks like a duck and quacks like a duck, don't mean it ain't a rooster."*

Chapter 9

The phone rang, awakening Montgomery. Zoren was dead to the world, snoring like an old VW. Figures! Montgomery thought. Zoren was the one who had insisted that they turn on the ringer in their room in case of a production emergency. Artier was at the hospital welcoming the new arrival to his ever growing brood, and would not be in to work.

Montgomery decided to let it go to voice mail. It was just after 5:00 am, and after having spent eighteen hours in the studio the night before, *nothing* in his opinion qualified as an emergency. He figured if it was that important, they would call back.

He rolled over to go back to sleep, when nature unrelentingly called. He untangled himself from the sheets and slid out of bed, his boxers barely restraining his morning hard-on. He staggered into the bathroom, hit the light, positioned himself at the toilet and jockeyed to keep from peeing on the floor. He freed himself from his boxers, leaving them behind on the floor and returned to bed where Zoren was still asleep in the pajama bottoms to the top he was wearing.

Montgomery religiously slept in a pajama shirt, winter or summer. If he didn't, he would undoubtedly wake up with a cold. He hated, however, sleeping in pajama bottoms, because they made him feel restricted. Zoren on the other hand, always slept in pajama pants. He especially liked the feel of silk ones rubbing against him. Conversely, he never slept with his upper body covered. Montgomery concluded that Zoren's back and chest were so hairy he didn't need to. Since they were about the same size, and neither of them slept in a complete set, they shared all their pajamas.

The sun spilled in through the blinds, illuminating Zoren's face. He stirred but not enough to make him conscious. His skin was an interesting blend of olive and caramel and as smooth as a baby's bottom. His black silky hair made him appear a lot darker than he actually was. Montgomery snuggled up next to him and gently kissed him on his eyelids. Women envied Zoren's lashes. The girls at the studio jokingly called him "Lasher Ross," which he thought was cute and harmless. Montgomery kissed him again. Zoren slowly opened his eyes.

"Do you remember the first time we met?

"What? What are you talking about?" Zoren said, still groggy.

"While I was watching you sleep, I was reminded of the day we met. Do you remember?"

"Of course I remember." Zoren said, sitting up and acclimating himself. "I'm the one who spotted you first."

"No, you didn't," Montgomery replied.

"I did. I came up to you at the taxi stand and said hello."

"Right! But I had already seen you at the currency exchange, and decided that although you were very good looking and inordinately sexy, I'd better get my luggage and figure out where the hell I was going to be staying."

"You've never told me that."

"And you think I tell you everything?" Montgomery said, smiling. Zoren got up and went into the bathroom.

"So, when I walked up to you at the taxi stand, you were just acting coy?" Zoren shouted from the bathroom.

"Coy? I was terrified. When I saw you at the currency exchange, you didn't look like the friendliest man in the world," Montgomery shouted back, "so when I turned around and found you standing there, I was a bit taken aback."

Zoren returned from the bathroom. "I didn't realize that you had given me that much energy."

"It wasn't all that, Zoren. Trust! You looked like a terrorist."

"A terrorist! I can't believe you said that."

"Well, it's what I thought."

"And exactly what does a terrorist look like?" Zoren asked, a little upset.

"Calm down, baby. You were a sexy terrorist," Montgomery joked.

"That ain't funny. It's just another example of how America propagates a bunch of negative bullshit about the rest of the world."

"Come on now, Zoren. I didn't think you were a terrorist, literally."

"Forget it!"

"Why you getting all mad?"

"I'm not mad!"

"Okay, then what else do you remember?"

"Everything, Montgomery. I remember everything."

"Then tell me!"

"I don't need to tell you. You were there."

"Come on, humor me?"

"Well, when I saw you standing there, you looked like you didn't know where in the world you were going."

"Zoren, how could I have looked like I didn't know where I was going? I was waiting for a damn taxi—at a taxi stand."

"You just did! Anyway, I thought you were very nice looking, and unlike you, I wasn't afraid to approach you."

"I did not say that I was afraid. I said finding a place to stay was a superior priority."

"Let's not fight about it."

"We aren't fighting."

"All I know is that I came up to you and said hello first."

"Okay, already. You get credit for that. You also said something about Michigan, which completely threw me off."

"I said you were either from Michigan or you had spent a significant amount of time there, and you asked me how I knew?"

"That's right, and you replied, 'I'm a dialect coach,' and I thought what the fuck is that? Which really didn't matter, 'cause you were fine as hell, and I was thinking, if this man is any indication of what this little European adventure has in store, I am off to a fabulous start. Then you actually went on to explain exactly what a fuckin' dialect coach was, as if I cared."

"I was just making conversation, and you seemed interested."

"I was, but not in what you did. After you thoroughly explained that you coached actors on perfecting specific dialects for television and film, you finally introduced yourself. 'I'm Zoren Ross,' you said, extending your hand, which I shook and discovered your grip to be very firm and very inviting."

"You know what. You need to stop!"

"No, really!"

"Montgomery, please!"

"My heart even skipped a few beats."

"Okay, if you say so."

"It did! And after I recovered."

"Honey stop it, you're being silly."

"No. This is the best part! After I told you my name, you replied, 'My pleasure,' and asked me if I was running away from someone or something. To which I replied, 'No, walk- ing!' You asked if you could walk with me and I said, 'sure, but I have no idea where I'm going.' Then you flashed that knee-buckling smile of yours and suggested that you help me figure it out—how convenient. I think it went something like, 'I'm between projects and I don't leave for Copenhagen for a few weeks. In the meantime, I'd be more than happy to show you around. How about we start by getting you a place to stay?' I said, 'sure,' and you went on, something about what my preference was."

"I said, 'What's your preference: Five Star, B&B, guest-house…?'"

"Zoren, please. You said, 'What's your preference,' trying to be cute. Then when I pretended not to get it, you came back with that Five Star, B&B, guest house shit, to which I replied, 'Guesthouse, preferably gay.' And you said, 'I thought so!'"

"To which I think that you were a little offended, honey."

"Why would I be offended?

"Because I'd clocked you."

"Clocked my ass, you hadn't clocked shit. I was on to you from giddy-up. If I was offended about anything, it was probably that you were being so presumptuous about me going to your guesthouse with you. Talking about, 'I'm stay-ing at Bromptons, a great little place in Earl's Court. I think you'll love it.'"

"If you knew what I was up to, why were you making it so damn difficult? Mr. 'I think I should probably get my own place.' Oh, and you were wrecked when I said, 'But you've misunderstood. I was suggesting that you might want to also stay at Bromptons, in your own accommodations of course.'"

"Which you lied about! 'Why don't you try Bromptons, and if it's not to your taste, I can certainly recommend something else. I know the area very well. But if it is satisfactory, then you'll be that much closer for dinner.' Now that I think back, that was so lame."

"But it worked! As a matter of fact, it was in that moment that I knew I had you."

"And what made you think that?"

"The look on your face, that said, o-kay!"

"Okay?"

"Yes! Okay Bromptons, okay dinner, okay whatever you want."

"So, that's why when we got to Bromptons you kept that little game up, huh? If I was so in and everything was so 'okay', why did you pretend that you didn't know they didn't have any availability? Suggesting that I stay the night with you, 'on the couch of course.' I knew that you knew all along that the guesthouse was booked."

"You did?"

"Yep!"

"Why didn't you say something?"

"It didn't matter, 'cause I was diggin' your terrorist ass, and I had already decided at the taxi stand that I was going to fuck you." Montgomery leaned over and gave Zoren a triumphant peck on the lips. At which time, he noticed the clock—5:10. "Oh shit, I've got to get my workout started," Montgomery said as he leapt from the bed.

"You don't have time for a little…you know? You take me on this trip down memory lane, get me all sizzling, then you want to run off to the gym. What's up with that?" Zoren said.

"After I'm done. I promise!" Montgomery replied, groping Zoren and giving him a long wet kiss.

The phone rang. Zoren reached for it. "Let the machine get it, baby," Montgomery said, "why don't you rustle us up some breakfast while I get my workout on."

"That sounds like a plan!" Zoren said grabbing his robe and heading for the kitchen.

Chapter 10

Zoren could hear the music coming from the gym as he attempted to prepare breakfast. He was actually a great cook, but with his schedule he hardly ever got into the kitchen, which was demonstrated by the difficult time that he was having trying to find anything. At the rate he was going, he thought it best that they dine out.

Artier prepared their meals and took care of the house. Both he and Montgomery realized how invaluable Artier was to their success, especially when he took a day off.

Montgomery was pumping hard at the squat rack when Zoren's voice came over the intercom, interrupting the music. "Are you almost finished, baby?"

"I've got one more exercise. Give me fifteen minutes."

"You've got ten."

"I need fifteen. I still need to shower."

"Skip the shower."

Montgomery quickly finished his last exercise and headed for the shower.

Breakfast was set up on the patio. It was a beautiful morning. Zoren had found his way around the kitchen well enough to have prepared what amounted to a feast, including scrambled eggs & cheese, grits, potatoes, bacon, sausage, and banana-nut waffles. He was sitting at the table in his favorite robe, enjoying his morning coffee and *Daily Variety* when Montgomery joined him, dressed in identical attire.

Matching robes with **H|R** monogrammed on them seemed like a wonderful idea when Montgomery bought them, unaware that they would become the source of endless disputes over who's was whose. He was certain that they were wearing each other's then, but he resolved that he wouldn't go there, especially since Zoren had been such a sweetheart and fixed a wonderful breakfast.

"Hey Boo, something sure smells good." Zoren smiled. He loved it when Montgomery called him Boo.

Boo sounded extra special, since their perpetual honeymoon had begun fourteen years ago to the day.

Monte joined Zoren at the table and lit a cigarette.

"I thought you quit smoking," Zoren said.

"I did. I just feel like one this morning."

"You're supposed to save it for after."

"I've got another one," Montgomery, kidded.

They enjoyed their breakfast, laughing and feeding each other like young lovers.

Zoren got up to get some more champagne. When he returned Montgomery was at the rail admiring the beautiful sky, the ocean crashing below, and the seagulls darting about. Zoren refilled their glasses and joined Montgomery at the rail. "Do you know the more I look at you, the finer you get?" Zoren said, planting a long wet kiss on Montgomery. (The kind of kiss that assured you that you weren't dealing with schoolboy inexperience.) Zoren returned to the table and Montgomery continued to gaze at the sky. "I think something is wrong with Max," he said.

"Why do you say that?"

"I just have this strange feeling."

"Why don't you call him."

"He's in Delhi. I'll have to call Gabby and find out what hotel he's at. It's probably nothing." Montgomery continued to admire the view.

"Honey!"

"What?" Montgomery replied, preoccupied.

"Come here," Zoren said. Montgomery turned to head toward the table where Zoren was sitting.

"Wait!" Zoren said.

"What?" Montgomery said puzzled.

"Leave the robe," he replied.

"But, I don't have anything on under it."

"Precisely!" Zoren smiled.

Montgomery untied his robe and let it fall to the ground. He proceeded to where Zoren was sitting. He climbed onto the table and crawled across it toward Zoren. The one thing

Montgomery loved more than Zoren's amazing sensitivity, was his desire to make money and freedom to make love any-and every-where. They'd had sex in the most inconceivable places, among them restaurant bathrooms, cathedrals, construction site port-a-johns, phone booths all over the world, and any other place they might be seen or caught. Mile-high Club members didn't have anything on them.

Zoren rose to give Montgomery an up close and personal view of his rapidly growing affiliate. Monte took it into his mouth and slowly down his throat. Zoren's package wasn't something you could take in one gulp; like cognac, you needed to let it glide down smooth and easy. Montgomery knew from experience, having gagged on it many times.

Once he felt Zoren's hoo-sack against his chin, he knew he was home free. He inhaled, taking in Zoren's obliging scent. He put his throat muscles to work, gently massaging Zoren's head.

"Damn, baby, that feels good," Zoren muttered. Montgomery responded by tightening up his throat just a little, keeping the throat massage up for as long as Zoren could take it.

When he felt Zoren beginning to tremble he worked hard to bring him home. Zoren couldn't take it. He grabbed Montgomery and pulled him off of him and kissed him deeply. He didn't want to cum yet. He wanted to bury himself deep inside Montgomery's tight ass.

He licked his way down Montgomery's body from his lips to his hips, stopping to give his nipples the proper attention.

Nipple play drove Montgomery completely wild. He loved to have them sucked, bitten, slapped and clamped. Zoren sucked and bit the right nipple while he gently slapped the left, increasing the intensity with each slap. Montgomery's dick throbbed.

Zoren descended to his knees and took Montgomery. He licked the shaft and swirled his tongue around the head and used his lips to suck him in deep. Montgomery grabbed the back of Zoren's head and started to thrust, being careful not to choke him. His sausage wasn't as big as Zoren's, but it wasn't to be underestimated. He picked up the tempo as Zoren's lips rode him like a well-greased piston. Montgomery warned that he was about to let off. Zoren knew that he had him. He pulled off, turned Montgomery around, and bent him over the table. He spread his cheeks and dove right for his freshly shaven ass, sucking and biting at the gate. He was thinking how nice it would have been to have Zoren shave him right there.

Zoren used his tongue like a key to unlock Montgomery's ass. Once inside, he replaced his tongue with one, two, then three fingers, but decided that he'd fist him another time. What he wanted was his "Johnson" buried deep in Montgomery's ass. He seized some butter from the table and lubricated himself. He stepped in close and positioned himself at the door. Zoren pushed in slowly, getting the head and about a third of the shaft pass the sphincter, without any protest from Montgomery. Preparation was everything. As he pushed in further, Montgomery's eyes rolled to the back of his head. "Ooooh, easy baby," he groaned.

"Open up for me, sweetheart." Zoren coaxed as he sunk it in to the hilt.

"Ooooooh shit, baby!"

Monte grabbed the sides of the table and clenched his teeth. "Shit! Take your time, Zoren." Zoren waited a few seconds while Montgomery's body adjusted to the intruder. He knew that with his size he couldn't just pile drive into Montgomery. Besides, he was trying to make love to his baby, not hospitalize him. He began to pump nice and slow. Montgomery bit down into his lower lip to keep from screaming, as the pain and pleasure soared in tandem through his body. There's nothing like being suspended in that realm between pain and pleasure, a feeling so intense that you're not sure if you're going to pass out, or lose your mind. Zoren picked up the pace and the pain converted to pure pleasure.

"Fuck me, dammit." Montgomery shouted. Zoren pumped harder.

"What's my name?" Zoren asked.

"Daddy," Montgomery replied.

Zoren loved to be called Daddy too. Boo was fine when it came to romance, but Daddy was the keyword when Montgomery wanted it full throttle.

Montgomery wasn't a passive player. He liked to get aggressive, particularly when he was the bottom. When

Zoren got close, Montgomery tightened up like a boa constrictor. Zoren couldn't move.

"You ain't doing nothin'," Montgomery teased.

"Oh, I ain't?" Zoren retorted.

"Nope!" With that said, Montgomery flipped over on his back, maintaining his grip. He wrapped his legs around Zoren's neck and said, "Now go for what you know, Daddy."

Zoren proceeded to plunge in and out, out and in, sweating like a marathon runner. After several minutes, he couldn't take anymore. He was ready to shoot, but he knew if he didn't put it on Montgomery like he liked it, he wasn't going to let him cum until he did, so he plunged in harder.

"That's how I like it, Daddy. That's it, put your back into it." Zoren finessed Montgomery like a seasoned pro. He pulled Montgomery's legs down and grabbed his shins, giving him the perfect angle to pound Montgomery's boy pussy to death.

"Oh shit, that's it!" Montgomery groaned. Without warning, Zoren stopped.

"Damn baby, don't do that! Come on, please, don't stop." Zoren pulled all the way out to the head, then plunged back in with one stroke, hitting Montgomery's prostate with a force that made them both shoot on contact.

He collapsed on top of Montgomery—spent. Tears rolled down the side of Montgomery's face. They lay there on the table in each other's arms, like they always did after they made love, thinking to themselves how lucky they were to have each other.

Montgomery's eyes were closed. The salt from the tears had stained the sides of his face. Zoren gently kissed him. "Have I told you that I love you today?" he asked. Without opening his eyes, Montgomery replied, "Yeah, when you were gettin' this—"

"Excuse me, telephone!" Jade interrupted.

"Don't you know how to knock, young lady?" Montgomery hollered embarrassed at the compromising position his daughter had found them—still intertwined on the table.

"This isn't exactly y'all's bedroom, Daddy," Jade replied, unfazed.

She had seen them both in various stages of undress before, and she had even seen them making love, although they weren't aware of it.

One morning they were getting it on in the weight room, when she accidentally walked in unnoticed. She hung around a minute and watched, before quietly slipping out. She actually admired how loving and free they were with each other, and hoped that one day she would be as lucky.

"Don't get smart with me, missy. Turn around," Montgomery said. Jade rolled her eyes and turned her head. They got up and put on their robes.

Jade was the product of what Maximillian called, "Montgomery's confused college days," when he had believed he was bisexual. Montgomery now fervently denied that he ever thought he was bisexual. He argued that he had merely been experimenting with women, and was never confused, nor thought himself to be bisexual, although his behavior might have suggested it.

Jessica, a girl in college that Montgomery had seen more off than on, between break-ups with his boyfriends, had become pregnant. He'd had mixed emotions about the pregnancy. He didn't mind becoming a father, but he did not want to marry Jessica. When he'd found out that she was pregnant, he'd already been back seeing Brad pretty seriously. Jessica had been heart-broken when he'd told her that he was in love with Brad and had no intentions of being with her.

She'd known that he dated men. He had told her in the very beginning, but like most girls, she'd believed it to be a phase and that eventually he would choose her. When Montgomery had refused, despite her pregnancy, she'd gone to his mother. She'd told Aprielle everything, including what details she knew of Montgomery and Brad's relationship. She'd hoped that Aprielle would insist that he marry her in order to avoid a scandal.

Aprielle had not been able to believe that Montgomery had been so stupid, but she'd not been ready to let the little indiscretion thwart his future. Jessica had agreed to be paid a handsome settlement upon termination of the pregnancy. Out of anger and humiliation, however, she'd reneged and gone into hiding until it was too late for an abortion, figuring that with an actual baby, maybe she'd be able to get an even bigger settlement.

When Jessica had resurfaced with her demands, Aprielle had laughed in her face and had had her sent away to a private facility, where she had been taken care of until the baby was born.

One afternoon, Aprielle had gotten a call and prepared to leave for what she'd called a business trip. Before her departure, she had insisted that Montgomery provide her with a blood sample. After a couple of days, she had returned with a gorgeous baby girl whom she called Jade.

Aprielle had informed Montgomery that Jade was indeed his daughter (not that he ever questioned it), and that she and Mr. H would be responsible for her. She never mentioned Jessica or the details of their arrangement. Jade had lived with her grandparents until, against everyone's advice, Montgomery had sued Aprielle for custody.

It had been a really unfortunate situation for Jade, having her father and grandmother fighting over her in court. After seven years, though, she seemed to have adjusted quite well to her new home. She and Aprielle continued to have a good relationship, despite the animosity between Aprielle and her father. Whenever they could, she and Aprielle spent time together traveling and shopping.

Chapter 11

"It's Gabby," Jade said, tossing the phone to her father and taking a seat at the table next to Zoren.

"Hey, Gabby. How are you?"

"I'm fine, sweetie. I've been trying to call you guys all morning. I was beginning to think that I had the wrong number."

"We heard the phone, but we were a little busy," he said. Zoren and Jade both laughed. They were so silly when they got together. Jade considered Zoren her best buddy. They spent a considerable amount of time together, playing tennis and video games, neither of which appealed to her father. He was often the one who helped her with class projects, and before she turned sixteen and got a car, he was the one who took her to and from school.

"Where is Artier?" Gabrielle asked.

"He's off today. His daughter had a baby last night. What's going on?"

"Things are kind of hectic around here," she said. He sensed in her voice that something was wrong. She wasn't her usual chipper self. He figured his mother had probably gotten on her nerves like she did everyone else's.

"You know I was going to call you this morning."

"Really?" she said.

"Yeah, I had the weirdest vision about Max."

"Oh?"

"Yeah, when I was looking out at the ocean this morning, I got a strong feeling that something was wrong. So I was planning to call you to get the number for the hotel he's staying in. Did Dad go on that safari? He actually wanted Max and me to go with him. Who in their right mind would wanna spend two weeks in the jungle?"

"That's exactly what your mother said."

"Huh?"

"Nothing. It doesn't matter."

"Hold on a minute, let me get a pen, so I can write that number down."

"Montgomery!" she said, sounding clearly like something was wrong.

"What's wrong Gabby?" he said, starting to get very concerned. Zoren and Jade looked on.

"Honey, I don't know how to tell you this."

"Just tell me what's wrong!"

"Sweetie, Max is dead. They found him in his office yesterday."

"Dead! Found who? Who's dead?"

"Who's dead?" Jade and Zoren asked.

"No! He's in Delhi."

"No, Baby. Your mother and Rico found him in his office."

The expression on his face said it all. Suddenly, joy was transformed into pain. Jade screamed, burying her face in Zoren's chest, realizing that her Uncle Max was the subject of the conversation. Zoren held her, rocking her and gently stroking her hair. Montgomery was trembling. Zoren pulled him to him and held them both, as they cried in his arms.

"Paul was found with him. It's all over the news. I know that you're going to be inundated with calls. The paper mentioned that you two were brothers."

"Are brothers, we are brothers!" He dropped the phone. Denial kicked in instantaneously. He couldn't comprehend it. He heard the words, but his brain kept saying syntax error. "We are brothers," echoed in his head like a mantra. Gabby called out his name over and over into the phone,

"Montgomery!"

"Montgomery!"

"Montgomery!"

He wasn't there. He had gone. The intensity of the pain he was experiencing transported him from his body to the driveway of the Hamilton property the day he and Maximillian were separated for the very first time.

Chapter 12

"Maaaax, hurry up, we're going to be late," Montgomery yelled to Maximillian, who had gone back upstairs to say goodbye to Jade. Montgomery told him that she was asleep, but he went anyway. He had a great big kiss for her, and an even bigger teddy bear that he had bought for her.

Montgomery had already said goodbye to his daughter the night before and presented her with a gold locket. Inside of it was a picture of him and Max. Unless Montgomery and Maximillian were in the room at the same time, Jade could not tell them apart. On the inside cover of the locket, he had had "Love, Daddy & Uncle Max" engraved. Maximillian loved Jade as much as Montgomery did, and was by far the more nurturing of the two.

Montgomery thought of how he was going to miss his baby girl. The last three months with her had been the best time of his life. She was absolutely adorable and looked just like he and Maximillian when they were little. The thought of not seeing her for a while made his pending plans all the more difficult.

Mr. Hamilton, Rico, and Montgomery were all gathered in the driveway hugging and kissing like they would never see each other again, while they waited on Maximillian. Aprielle was nowhere to be found—not that anyone expected her. She had done her part by executing the grandest, almost spectacle, farewell party you could imagine. She would, of course, expect a call from the boys once they arrived in Boston, to thank her for the new roadsters they would find when they got there. Surprising her boys with gifts was one of her greatest joys, though if you were to ask Montgomery, he'd say it was her way of trying to control them.

Gabrielle watched the farewells from her window. She had a one hundred and eighty-degree view of the property, which enabled her to see the wooded area behind the house, everyone's comings and goings, and Rico's morning swim, the one that still got her all hot and bothered.

The usual activities at the Hamilton house were on hiatus. The Hamilton boys were off to Harvard Law School (Montgomery) and Harvard Medical School (Maximillian). At least that's what everyone thought, until Montgomery dropped the bomb.

Gabby hurried down to say goodbye. Rico asked her to come along so she could keep him company on the drive back. She figured Aprielle wouldn't be up for a while, so she did. Mr. Hamilton decided that they should go on without him. He wanted to say his goodbyes right there and save himself some predictable embarrassment at the airport.

He told Montgomery that Brad had called to wish him luck and say goodbye. Montgomery had given every one in the house strict instructions regarding Brad's calls: basically, he didn't want to talk to him.

Montgomery and Mr. Hamilton had been debating the merits of Brad all summer. Mr. Hamilton liked Brad and thought that Montgomery was being cruel. Aprielle, on the other hand, was as pleased as punch that after two years, Montgomery's "friend," as she had labeled him, was at last no longer in the picture. Although she never talked about the relationship one way or the other, she had definite feelings about it, and they were not the feelings of Mr. Hamilton.

Maximillian returned, gave his father a hug and a kiss, and proceeded to get into the car. As they were getting into the car to leave, Mr. Hamilton started in with his fatherly advice, which both boys thought was pretty sappy.

"Montgomery, be careful not to trample people's hearts. Whether it be Brad, David, or whomever, remember son, people have feelings."

"Yeah, alright," Montgomery replied. Maximillian stood up through the sunroof to get his pearls of wisdom.

"Maximillian, take care of your brother. Help keep him focused. I love you boys with all my heart," Mr. Hamilton said.

"We love you too!" they impatiently replied in perfect unison, and closed the door.

Before the car was out of the driveway, Maximillian turned on the stereo and opened a bottle of champagne, filled two glasses, and passed one to Montgomery. As if there could be any party left in either of them after the night before. Maximillian raised his glass and began a toast, "To the future Maximillian P. Hamilton, M.D. and Montgomery P. Hamilton, Esquire." "To freedom," Montgomery mumbled to himself, preoccupied with his thoughts. Max emptied his glass in one gulp, poured himself another, and turned up the music.

"Would you please turn that down. I have a headache," Montgomery said. He didn't really have a headache. He just had a lot on his mind and was not in the mood for the party atmosphere that Maximillian was determined to create. Undaunted by Montgomery's withdrawal, Maximillian continued his makeshift party. "Drink up Monte. It'll help your headache, man," Maximillian said, trying to pep Montgomery up.

"Turn that fuckin' music down and grow up."

"What is your problem?"

"I told you I have a headache."

"So you're going to make my life miserable? Is this about Mother? What do think she's done to you this time?"

"This is not about her." He paused. "Max, if you could be anything in the world, what would it be?"

"The son of Aprielle Hamilton. What else is there?"

"Be serious."

"I am serious. How many young brothers do you know who, live like we do?"

Maximillian was serious. The average black man, young or old, didn't move through the world as they did. It wasn't because they were educated, either; many black men had become educated. It was because their mother was rich and connected, plain and simple.

"Come on Max, indulge me."

"Okay, a Playboy."

"What?"

"A Playboy, you know, traveling the world racing fast cars and fast women, hanging with Hugh up in the mansion."

"Forget it! You can't be serious for one damn minute?" Montgomery said.

"I'm telling you, I am serious. The way the ladies be after me." Montgomery had to laugh. He knew he wasn't going to get anything out of Maximillian. He was having a good time, and all he was looking forward to was finishing medical school and assuming his place as successful son of Aprielle Hamilton.

Montgomery dug around in his bag looking for his comb. "Have you seen my comb?" he asked Maximillian.

"What do I look like? I don't keep up with your comb. You need to cut that long ass shit off anyway. It's dated, looking like some crazy ass revolutionary, and you ain't got shit to revolt about." Maximillian shook his head.

Montgomery was the proverbial rooter for the underdog. He had never really been comfortable having more than others. Although he loved nice things, he didn't like the separation and conflict that often occurred when you had things that others didn't. When he was little he was always giving things away to cousins and others who didn't have as much as him. When he became older he expressed his discomfort by volunteering at various charities.

When he was eight years old, in middle school, he and Maximillian went on a field trip to the Downtown Mission to feed the homeless. Montgomery felt so sorry for them, that every year at Thanksgiving he begged Greta to fix something special for him to take down to the mission. Rico took him, until he thought he was old enough to go by himself on his motor scooter. When he was twelve or thirteen he was mugged and his scooter was taken on his way home from the mission. When Aprielle found out about it, she was furious. She forbade him from going down there by himself. She told him if he insisted on going to feed the homeless, to have Rico take him and wait for him.

"Are you ready to answer my question?" Montgomery asked.

"What's the question?" Maximillian replied.

"If you could be anything in the world, what would it be?"

"What are you talking about? I'm on my way to being what I want to be—"

"What? A doctor with a world famous practice, ultimately pioneer something, and become the first Black man to do it," Montgomery interrupted, frustrated.

"Damn skippy!" Maximillian replied.

"But isn't that her dream? Is that what you really want?"

"Yes, it's what I really want. It's my dream."

"You sure 'bout that?"

"Yes, Monte. Why are you asking me these crazy ass questions? So what if it started out as her dream. What's wrong with that? If anything, she just planted the seed, that's all. I'm the one doing all the work. You need to have you a drink and chill, little brother."

Montgomery wondered how they could look so much alike and yet be so different, it had to be those twenty four minutes. They saw the world through completely different eyes, but as different as they were, they were completely connected to one another emotionally. Montgomery opened the Jack Daniels and poured himself a real drink.

"I've been thinking a lot about my life lately, and I really think I want to pursue something other than law," Montgomery said. He couldn't believe how uncomfortable he was actually verbalized it. He had been thinking about it for a long time, but had never actually said it to anyone.

"Like what?" Maximillian asked.

"Radio," he replied, waiting for Maximillian's reaction. They both knew how their mother felt about Blacks being entertainers. It was fine for those who couldn't do anything else, but her sons had too many tools at their disposal. She would rather them live off of her than entertain folks, especially White folks.

"A radio personality, actually." Montgomery said.

"A what?"

"A radio personality, like—"

"A damn disc jockey? Have you lost your mind? You really do need to cut that hair off your head. It is apparently clogging up your brain. I can see you now, sitting in some little fishbowl, spinning records and doing traffic reports." Maximillian said, laughing. "Not exactly how I would have envisioned your future, baby brother. I would have put my money on you becoming something a little more noteworthy."

"No, not a disc jockey. Not that there's anything wrong with being a disc jockey. I'm talking about a talk radio host. Someone who facilitates discussions about societal and political issues." He was defensive. He was hoping that Maximillian would have been more supportive.

"Yeah, whatever, and when you're tired of that after two weeks, then what?" Maximillian was reminding Montgomery of his endless tangents. Like the undergraduate-year summer when he decided he wanted to become a Marine. He went and signed up, then changed his mind. His mother had to pull some strings to keep them from making him keep his commitment, and get him back in school.

"You're going to finish law school, then do local politics, and I don't mean talking about it on the radio, I mean become Michigan's first Black Governor or something, and maybe even one day have a shot at the Presidency."

"Why would I want to be President, Max? Do you really think I'm aspiring to be some off-screen actor serving the public a bunch of Oscar award winning bullshit, and not have a chance at one of those little statues. I thought you knew me better than that."

"You would be a great politician. You're always trying to make a difference. There's your opportunity to really make a difference."

"Max, I cannot believe that you're that naive. Politicians don't have any real power. Politicians are public servants, that's right, servants, servants whose power lies with lobbyist and special interest groups who buy and sell their two-faced plastic asses every day. Now wouldn't mother love that! Sorry, big brother, I have no desire to be a fuckin' puppet or play daddy to this racist nation. You've apparently confused Mother's desires with mine."

"You are crazy!"

"Man, we have all this material shit, and what does it mean, that some bitch will throw some pussy at us, or some motherfucker will be our friend, because they think we have something that they don't."

"We do!"

"No we don't. It just seems like we do. I want to help people see that they have what it takes to create this same shit, if that's what they want. Our mother isn't exactly a rocket scientist, you know. She was simply a determined woman with a vision, a plan, and no intention of letting anyone or anything get in her way.

"Most people don't do much, because they don't know that it's possible. I see radio as a way to help others understand the possibilities. In the next ten years, you watch, mass communication is going to dominate this culture. I believe it will be the primary vehicle for reaching and shaping the thinking of the American public. You mark my words."

"What about law school?"

"What about it?"

"Where does it fit in this new vision of your future?"

"It doesn't. That's why I'm not going."

"What do you mean you're not going? I don't know why you're talking all this pie in the sky shit. You've been a Hamilton long enough to know how the game is played. In case you've forgotten, let me remind you. All you got to do is get that damn degree, graduate somewhere in the top five percent, shit, ten percent of your class, and you're set, for-ever. I don't know about you, but I'm not blowing any sweet ass deal like that. What's so hard about that? Why can't you get with the program?"

"Because it's not my fuckin' program," Montgomery shouted, "Do you realize our futures have been planned for us since the womb? So far things have gone according to plan, with the exception of a few indiscretions on my part, which our wonderful mother promptly took care of. All in all, I'd say we are on course. If you have been paying atten-tion to anything I have said, you would know this is not pie in the sky shit I'm talking."

"Ok, let's play this out. We are on our way to the airport to catch a plane to Boston and you are talking about becom-ing a disc jockey. What am I missing?"

"I am trying to tell you I am not going to Boston, Max. I am going to Europe." "What!?" Maximillian threw up his hands, exasperated.

"What about Jade? So, you're just going to leave her?"

"You mean what about you, don't you?"

"I meant what about Jade, just like I said, but since you brought it up, what about me?"

"I'll always be here for you."

"How are you going to be here for me, there?"

"Space won't change that. I'll always be here for you, there for you, whatever it takes. In case your original question was sincere, Mom'll take care of Jade like she does everything else. She thinks she's hers anyway." Maximillian buzzed Rico and Gabby. Rico lowered the partition.

"What's up, fellas?" Rico said.

"Monte is back here trippin'. He claims that he's not going to Boston…"

"There's been a slight change of plan," Montgomery interjected. "You should drop Max off at United, as planned. I, however, need to make a little pit stop and join him in Boston later in the week. I need some space to think."

"Stop lying, you said you were going to Europe, not making a pit stop."

Maximillian suddenly looked terrified. He realized that Montgomery was not kidding.

"What are you up to, Montgomery?" Gabby asked.

"A little adventure. That's all. I'll tell you all about it later."

"That's okay! I don't want to know about it—that way if your mother asks me anything, I don't have to lie. Look at your brother." Maximillian was visibly shaken.

"He'll be alright. He can handle it."

Montgomery began gathering up his things as Rico approached the terminal. Maximillian was urgently trying to figure out what to say or do to make Montgomery stay.

"That's fucked up, man! You don't care about anybody but yourself," he said—a final and desperate attempt to get through to Montgomery.

"What are you talking about? I care about you."

"You've always been like that. I don't know why I'm surprised. You do this shit to everybody."

"Do what?"

"Make completely selfish decisions, with no consideration for anyone but yourself. You did it to Jessica; you did it to Jason; you did it to Brad, and now you're doing it to me and your daughter."

"That's not true. I was never committed to any of them."

"Of course, not!"

"I wasn't. We were just having fun. Jessica didn't give a shit about me, all she saw were dollar signs; and Jason, he and I were fuck buddies. I had always made that crystal clear. He tried to turn it into something else. As for Brad, Brad was a weak little boy. I actually thought that he and I might have been able to make it, but I need a man, not a little boy."

"I hate you. You try to justify every fuckin' thing that you do. Well, I tell you what, if you get out of this car, you will no longer be my brother. You can consider yourself dead, and we'll see how you figure out how to justify that."

Rico pulled up to the airport terminal and popped the trunk.

"I hope you don't mean that," Montgomery said.

"I do!"

"That's unfortunate." Montgomery prepared to get out of the car. "Take care of yourself Max, and don't let the ladies take your mind off your books." He stuck his hand out. Maximillian ignored it.

"Here, this is for you," Montgomery said, handing Maximillian a package from his bag.

"I don't want that!" Maximillian threw the package at him. "How long have you been planning this?"

"Max, take it."

"I don't want it! Answer my question: how long have you been planning this?"

"I've been thinking about it for a while, but I really didn't decide until this very moment. I am not trying to hurt you. This is so fucking hard for me, but it's something I have to do, for me. I love you and I hope you'll try to understand. I have to go, or I'm going to end up missing my flight. Take care of yourself. I will call you as soon as I get there."

Maximillian turned his head away. Montgomery reached to try to hug him. Maximillian pushed him away with such force that he hit his head on the window.

"What the hell's wrong with you?!" Montgomery screamed. Maximillian did not respond.

"Say it. Say it, dammit." Montgomery shouted at him. Maximillian was like a stone. Montgomery broke down. With tears streaming down his face, he begged Maximillian, "Please say it. Say you loved me first. I'm not trying to hurt you. I'm sorry, I am so sorry. I really need to hear you say it."

"All I have to say is, consider yourself dead." Montgomery lowered his head. He could not believe that Maximillian had refused to say what had been their call and response since they were three years old.

It had started as a way to make up after a fight. One afternoon, Gabrielle had overheard them arguing back and forth. Maximillian had said, "I love you" to Montgomery, who had replied, "I loved you first." To which Maximillian had replied, "Unt un, I loved you first, 'cause I loved you in Mommy's stomach." They had gone back and forth until they had started hitting each other. Gabrielle had thought it was the cutest thing for them to be literally fighting over who loved whom more.

She had stopped them from fighting and told them that they should never forget how much they loved each other. Whenever they had a little fight or disagreement, they should be sure to remind each other of just how much they loved one another. As they grew up, it became their greeting and farewell. No matter how mad they got with each other, it always brought them back together.

Montgomery got out of the car. He turned back, his eyes red and swollen. He said it one last time, "I love you."

"May you rest in peace," Maximillian replied, and closed the door. Montgomery mumbled to himself the reply Maximillian refused to give to him, "I loved you first," and disappeared into the airport.

Later, he would drink himself to sleep, having realized that something died between them, something he had never expected.

Chapter 13

Mr. H finally arrived home, in terrible shape. He collapsed in the chair before taking his coat and hat off. "Gabrielle, how is she?" he asked, referring to Aprielle.

"She seems to be okay. She's in bed resting right now. Dr. Oatis gave her a sedative, which has her pretty much out of it. She found him, you know," I said.

"That's what they told me, she and Rico. What happened?"

"We don't know anything yet," I replied. I was in the process of making myself some tea when he came in. I prepared a cup for him as well and went to help him out of his coat, which he had made no attempts to take off.

"Gabby, I was always away," he said, his eyes welling up.

"What do you mean?" I asked.

"I wasn't there when they were born. Remember, I was in Seattle, and by the time I got to the hospital they were already here. I wasn't there to welcome him like a real dad and I wasn't here to say goodbye."

"Don't beat yourself up; none of us got to say goodbye. Max loved you and so does Monte. Let me get you some tea."

"Gabby, I prayed so hard for them. On our honeymoon, Aprielle told me ours would be a childless union. When I told her she should have told me this before, she suggested I file for an annulment. She said she had plans and mother-hood was not in them. Gabby, I knew she was career minded and all, but it had never occurred to me that she didn't want children. I was deeply disappointed and for a fleeting moment I considered filing, but I truly loved her, as I still do. At that time, women weren't like Aprielle. She was in a class all by herself. Her clarity about she wanted and her determi-nation to get it was what drew me to her and made me fall in love with her. I accepted the situation, but I never stopped praying that one day she would change her mind, and make me a father."

"How did you finally get her to change her mind?"

"I didn't. God intervened. In the summer of 1960, he stepped in and answered my prayers.

"Aprielle had been feeling under the weather and after a series of tests, nothing was revealed. Since Dr. Oatis couldn't find anything from the various tests he had run, he sug-gested a pregnancy test, which we both thought was ludi-crous. First, she was almost forty years old, and second, she had had a tubal ligation several years before. Because it was a relatively new procedure, she was always extremely careful. We never had relations just before or after she ovulated, and she still used her diaphragm, or I wore a condom. There was no way she was pregnant.

"She called me and asked me to join her at the condo in New York. I was here in Michigan. She said that she had something very important to tell me. I thought it was about her new cosmetic line or something. Whenever she was contemplating a new product, she would ask my opinion about it over dinner.

"When I arrived, there was a wonderful candlelight dinner, and music playing. We ate and were relaxing, enjoying our after dinner drinks. She sat up erect, as if preparing herself for something serious. I figured she was about to tell me about the new product she was considering. Instead, she told me that she was pregnant. She just came right out with it, 'Hamilton, I'm pregnant.' I'll never forget that moment; time as we know it stopped. I just sat there staring at her in disbelief.

"She said that she had had the pregnancy test done purely to shut Dr. Oatis up. When the test had come back positive, she had been sure that there had been some kind of mistake, so she didn't bother to tell me. She then had the test redone a second, and a third time. They all had confirmed that she was indeed pregnant. I immediately started thanking God. It was the happiest moment of my life."

He started to tear up. I handed him a Kleenex. He wiped his face and continued. "She wasn't happy at all, Gabby. Actually, she was very cold. She said she did not know why I was crying, she should be the one crying, since it was the absolute worst time for her to have to be away from the office.

"She had already made arrangements to go the Orient to have an abortion. I was furious. I told her she had no right to kill our baby. It was one thing to waste my seed, but kill our baby, that was not her right. I didn't understand how she could even consider having our child ripped out of her. I forbade her. I told her, 'You will not have an abortion, I forbid you, and that's final.' She blew up and started screaming, 'Until you can get pregnant, carry a baby to term, and manage having your life turned completely upside down, Cyrus, you better get out of my face, and you don't forbid me from doing anything.' When putting my foot down—as much as I could with her—didn't work, I resorted to plain old begging. She said she was going to write Congress and tell them it did not make any sense for her to have to spend the kind of money it was costing her to go to halfway around the globe, for a procedure that should be made safe and legal in what was supposed to be the greatest country in the world.

"The day she was to leave for the procedure, she got up early and had a long hot bath. I joined her for breakfast with a big box, and an even bigger smile. She opened the box, which had another, very small, Tiffany box inside. Inside the Tiffany box was a 24-karat gold pendant with "Mother" spelled in diamonds. I had had it especially made for her. I'd hoped it would stir her motherly instinct, and she would change her mind. She said, 'Oh, Hamilton, this is beautiful, but I can't. I do not know anything about being a mother, and besides, I am too old.' I told her that we could hire somebody to help. I even promised to help. I meant that Gabby, I really did. I didn't know anything about being a father either, but I was willing to try. I begged her, 'Please don't go through with this.' She said, 'I'm sorry, Hamilton, I can't.'

"She gave me the box back, went and got her sweater, and told Rico she wanted to leave for the airport right away, although her flight didn't leave for another six hours."

How horrible, I thought. Just then, Aprielle came down the stairs into the kitchen where Mr. H and I were sitting.

"Hamilton, when did you get back?" she asked, and gave him a hug. She was still a little groggy. "Is there any more hot water? Where's Greta?"

"I'll get you some," I said. I poured her some tea and refreshed our cups as well.

"My ears were burning. I knew somebody, somewhere, was talking about me. What tales is he down here telling you?"

"He was just telling me about when you found out you were pregnant with the boys."

"Oh my, did he say that I was a cold-hearted, corporate-climbing bitch with no motherly instinct?"

"No!"

"She knows I would never say that," he interjected. "I was telling her about the pendant I gave you from Tiffany's at breakfast and how you gave it back, because you said you couldn't."

"I couldn't, Gabrielle. I was a businesswoman. I had always seen myself that way, even when I was a little girl. I had never envisioned myself as a mother. I could not run a corporation and be an effective mother. More women today are realizing that they cannot do it all, although most of them are still pretending that they can. That is why their children are all messed up."

"I have to agree with you there," I said.

"Gabrielle, that was one of the hardest decisions I ever had to make. Men cannot understand. They never have to come face to face with that choice. I had a new company to run and nurture, there was not enough to go around, so an abortion was the best decision. Not that it was an easy decision, but all things considered, the intelligent choice. Did he tell you that I left six hours early for the airport?"

"Yes," I said. She smiled and shook her head in disbelief at her own behavior.

"I hated to see him in so much pain, it tore me apart. I did not want to hurt Hamilton. He had always been my biggest supporter and I felt like I was letting him down, but I also knew he didn't understand. He said that he'd help, but he was always on the road. That was his ego talking. He wasn't even there when they were born, if you remember."

"I wanted to be," he interjected.

"I know you did. We want a lot of things, but I've always preferred having a little of the best, as opposed to a whole lot of mediocrity. I believe you felt that somehow you were less of a man, because you had not made a baby. I remember pouring myself a scotch in the back of the car, thinking that. Then I concluded that technically, you had made one, we just weren't keeping it."

"There may be some truth to that, but inside I really did want to be a father."

"Well, what made you change your mind?" I asked her.

"Well, when I got to the airport I had all this time on my hands, so I decided to browse the magazines and books. It seemed like every title I saw was about babies and mother-hood, but my mind was made up, and I was not about to let a few magazine titles change my mind. I was too busy think-ing about how I could turn this truly inconvenient situation into a little retreat. It had been a long time since I had had time to just relax, so I figured it a perfect opportunity to have some time to myself, do a little shopping, and get a whole lot of pampering.

"I heard my flight being called: *We're now boarding all first class passengers and those passengers needing special assistance for flight 419 to Singapore.* I thought, '419: that is my birth date—it must be an omen.' I hurried to a nearby payphone to call Rico, so he could call my Uncle Buster, who ran numbers, and put it in for me, straight and boxed, both races for a hundred dollars. I had come a long way from April Louise Johnson, but I was not going to pass up playing a hunch when I got one. Besides, it was no different from going to Las Vegas, maybe a little less glamorous, but gam-bling just the same.

"As I hung up with Rico, I heard my name being called over the paging system: *Aprielle Hamilton, please pick up the blue courtesy phone, conveniently located in the terminal.* I thought, 'What in the world?' I found the bank of telephones. Of course there were no blue ones. I thought, 'Now wouldn't it make good sense to put a blue phone with the payphones?'"

"Of course not, that would have been too much like right." I said.

"So, by the time I found the blue courtesy phone, which may have been blue but certainly was not conveniently located, the operator informed me that there had been a man there, who said that he was my husband, but had left to find me himself. Just as I hung up with the operator, Hamilton comes running toward me with a couple dozen roses, about to keel over from exhaustion. Gabrielle, he got right down on his knees in the middle of the airport. I said, 'Cyrus, would you please get up from there, you are embarrassing me.'"

"You know she only calls me Cyrus when she's irritated," he interjected.

"I'm trying to tell the story, Hamilton," she asserted. "Now Gabrielle, he would not move. I was so embarrassed. He was on the floor, tears running down his face, begging. 'Aprielle, please don't do this. I love you so much. We can work this out. I know we can. In all our years together, I haven't asked for very much. I've been both understanding and supportive of everything you've ever wanted to do.

Many times I didn't agree with you and sometimes I didn't understand, but I trusted you. I followed your lead.'

"A crowd had begun to form around us. I was beyond embarrassed then. He kept going on. 'Can't you find it in your heart to trust me on this one. I know you're scared. That's the only reason you're doing this. Sweetheart, if it's any consolation, I'm scared too, but please, just this one time, I'm asking you. Will you follow my lead?' I said, 'Yes, if it will get you up off of the floor, yes!'

"The crowd started whistling and cheering. I took the flowers and helped him up. I said, 'You are too old for this Hamilton, you look ridiculous.' So, to answer your question, I guess sheer embarrassment is what changed my mind."

"So, it had nothing to do with me?" Mr. H asked.

"Of course not Darling, it is always about me," she winked at him. "Now come on upstairs so I can tell you all about what I have planned for the service. I'm thinking about white doves and a gray color scheme. Maximillian loved gray."

"He loved blue," Mr. H said.

"Oh well, we'll go with gray anyway," she replied. She took him by the arm to lead him upstairs. I handed him another cup of tea to take with him. They were so cute together. The sedative was apparently wearing off. She was returning to her old self. I had wanted to talk to him about the journal, but decided it could wait.

Three Days Later

Chapter 14

When we arrived at the church, the news trucks were already setting up. They were determined to turn our private pain into a public spectacle. The service wasn't scheduled to begin for another five hours. Aprielle had asked me to go over and make sure that everything was in order. Rico accompanied me so that I wouldn't have to face the situation alone.

While Rico was talking with one of the drivers, I wandered into the church and found myself in the very situation that he was supposed to be there to help me avoid. I was instantly covered with goose bumps from my scalp to my heels. I was shivering out of control. I entered the sanctuary. A war broke out between my shivers and tears. My tears became rivers as I wept openly; however, I can say I was safely on this side of the distraught-colored-woman-at-a-funeral routine. You know the one that begins with some big woman—for some reason, they're always big—screaming at the top of her lungs, "Oh my baby, not my baby," followed by "Jesus, why me? Why me, Lord? You might as well just take me too. I can't live without him." And then out of nowhere she dives for the coffin. By the time she's finally brought under control, the corpse is half out the box, flowers are everywhere, her slip is showing, wig is twisted, shoes are missing, and five nurses and ten spectators are fanning her. This was not my style—besides, that type of performance requires an audience.

When I reached the casket, I felt a profound peace. He looked wonderful. Once the sedative Dr. Oatis had given Aprielle had worn off, she went right to work on the arrangements, hiring a team of coordinators, an award-winning lighting director, and a choir from Los Angeles. She insisted that everything be perfect. Mr. Hamilton said that after fifty-something years of marriage, she'd finally achieved the ultimate in sterile and impersonal. Despite opinions about Aprielle's way—and there were many—one thing was unarguable: her results were spectacular.

The color scheme was shades of gray, from baby soft pastel to electric steel. A spray of white roses and tiger lilies topped the casket. Hundreds of individually caged white doves were placed at the entrance, awaiting release at the conclusion of the service. Swanson's had done a remarkable job in preparing him. Every corpse I'd ever seen always looked rubbery, way too dark, and very dead.

They had matched his complexion precisely, his hair was cropped just the way he liked it, and his nails were buffed, not polished, which was always his preference. His wedding band shimmered in the light. He was wearing his favorite navy blue suit. Mr. Hamilton had insisted that he be put away in a suit of his favor, and the sentimentality of it being a gift from Montgomery made it all the more personal. He looked as dashing and radiant in death as he had in life.

The choir's musicians were setting up. I went over their instructions with them. They were to move immediately into *Don't Cry For Me* the moment the family appeared in the sanctuary entrance.

Aprielle had flown the choir in from California. It was a choir that she had seen in an Arco commercial a few years ago. She found out whom they were, and that they were based in Los Angeles. She flew there many times especially to hear them, and never missed the opportunity to hear them whenever she was in Los Angeles on business. She would call Jade, they would meet at service, and afterward they'd have brunch and go shopping.

The pastor of the church where the choir was from had been a guest on Montgomery's show, and the two of them had become fast friends, so occasionally he and Zoren had visited.

One Sunday, they'd walked in and there was Aprielle perched up on the front pew. She would always sit down front so the Reverend could acknowledge her. Monte and Zoren had come and sat right next to her. During the Reverend's acknowledgement of visitors, Montgomery had pointed to her and mouthed to the Reverend that she was his mother. The Reverend had made a big deal out of it by saying, "Saints, we have some very special people in God's house today. America's own Montgomery Hamilton-Ross, star of—I don't need to tell you—Saints you know who he is, and the other half of television's hottest duo, Zoren Hamilton-Ross, and all the way from the Motor City, please give a Christian welcome to Ms. Cosmetics herself, the sisters know who I'm talking about, and some of the brothers, Amen—Aaaamen! Stand up, Sister Hamilton. Now you mean to tell me all these times you've popped in on us, you haven't ever told us that you're this boy's momma? We're always honored to have him and Zoren visit us. They do some wonderful things for the community.

"Show all our visitors some love church, Amen." Montgomery had told me that Aprielle had smiled politely and assumed the posture of the proud mother, but he knew she had not been happy about being put on the spot like that. He'd said that before service was over she had slipped out.

I felt Rico's presence next to me and turned to find him wiping away his tears. He and Maximillian had become very close, especially after Montgomery had left for Europe. I suggested that we get back, so we could get ready. We both agreed that Aprielle's expectations had been met, if not exceeded.

Chapter 15

The church was filled to capacity, in both the main sanctuary, which seated five thousand, and the overflow rooms where the service could be seen on big screen television. Hundreds of people remained outside, unable to gain entry. Aprielle had timed our arrival perfectly. The program was scheduled to begin at eleven o'clock. The service was to open with a processional. She figured that with all the people expected to attend, the processional would take about two hours, therefore, the family should arrive around one o'clock.

Camille's car met us at the house, so that the family cars could follow each other to the church, and we would arrive together. When we arrived, we had to fight through a swarm of reporters to get to the door. It took about ten minutes or so to get through the sea of reporters and news cameras. We remained silent, hiding our pain and disgust behind our dark glasses, and Aprielle behind a huge hat that practically concealed her entire face.

The choir changed selections on cue as we made our way toward the casket for the final viewing. Camille, who was carrying Madison and holding tightly to little Max's hand, suddenly became hysterical, bucking and crying out Maximillian's name, pleading for the Lord to take her too.

I should have known that Camille would provide the drama *de rigueur*, classifying the service as a bona fide Negro funeral. Two buxom uniformed nurses struggled to calm her down. They tried to help her to her seat. Aprielle was appalled by Camille's lack of decorum. Rico and I took the children.

Aprielle, who was tearlessly composed, and Mr. Hamilton made their way to the casket. Mr. Hamilton could barely keep his balance. She took one of the white roses from the spray and placed it inside. She slid slightly to her right and allowed for she and Mr. Hamilton to be photographed by the one non-flash photographer that had been permitted to photograph the service, provided that no pictures were taken of the deceased. Mr. Hamilton seemed almost catatonic. His legs threatened to give way. He couldn't believe that he was saying goodbye to the son he had prayed so hard to get. He wept. His tears dropped softly onto Max's lapel. Aprielle handed him the handkerchief from his breast pocket. She tried to hold him up as best she could, but she had to motion for one of the nurses to come and assist them to their seats.

Once Rico and I got the children calmed down, we took them up to say their final farewell to their father.

"Is Daddy sleeping, Auntie Gabby?" Madison asked.

"He's not sleeping, silly," Max Jr. interjected, "he's in heaven. Ain't that right, Auntie Gabby?"

"That's right, darling," I said.

Aprielle and Camille had argued over whether the children should have attended. Camille insisted that they go. Her position was that children shouldn't be sheltered from everything, that it was more important for things to be explained to children in terms that they could understand, and she was perfectly capable of doing that. It was a rare occasion when I agreed with Camille and that happened to be one of them. I was confident that Camille would handle the children's questions and concerns appropriately, but after she fell out at the church, I can't say that I was as confident.

I wondered if Montgomery was going to make it. I inquired with the funeral director for what must have seemed to him like the hundredth time. I asked him to be sure to keep an eye out for him. I reminded him that Montgomery was an exact replica of the deceased, and instructed him to escort him immediately to the family seating, ignoring any resistance.

I had tried to call Montgomery earlier that morning, but hadn't gotten an answer. I was hoping that he wouldn't decide not to come. I knew Montgomery had a mind of his own and didn't stand on ceremony. Even though it was the worst of circumstances (in fact it was precisely because of the circumstances), I wanted to lay my eyes on him. So much had happened and so much had changed since he and Zoren had unexpectedly shown up at the Waterfront Pediatric Center opening.

Chapter 16

"The honorable Mayor Coleman A. Young" was announced over the public address system. Aprielle quickly made her way to the entrance. Maximillian was right behind her.

Having the guests announced as they arrived allowed her to mingle, making sure that Maximillian chatted up all the right people, while still being able to provide immediate attention to the more distinguished guests as they arrived. I was covering the door for Camille, who had gone to the ladies room, when Mayor Young walked in. Although Camille was the other managing doctor, her job that night was to play hostess.

"Coleman, darling, I am so glad that you could make it," Aprielle said, extending her hand for him to kiss.

"I wouldn't have missed this for the world," he said as he kissed her hand. "I can't believe that he's old enough to even be a doctor. And you, a doctor's mother, why you don't look old enough to be anyone's mother."

"Coleman, that kind of pre-election flattery is sure to get you re-elected," she smiled, air kissing him and locking her arm in his.

"Where you been, old man?" Mr. Hamilton said as he walked over, greeting the mayor with an enthusiastic handshake. "Haven't seen you at the club lately. Been hiding, huh?"

"Hiding? I have a six o'clock tee time in the morning. You be there and bring your A-game," the mayor replied.

"I always bring my A-game. You better make sure you bring yours."

"Now, gentlemen," Aprielle interrupted, "enough of that. Tonight, all conversation should be about the Maximillian P. Hamilton Waterfront Pediatric Center and the good doctor himself. Why Coleman, you haven't even congratulated the medical community's new crowned prince. Maximillian, honey, you remember Mayor Young," she said, turning the focus back to the business of the evening.

"Of course. Good evening, Mr. Mayor," Maximillian said.

"Your chest ought to be pretty puffed up, young man. This is place is amazing."

"Thank you, sir. The credit should actually go to my mother," Max replied.

"Nonsense," she said, gloating and clutching the mayor's arm.

Awe-inspiring is the only way to describe the place. It was surrounded by water and had an atrium that gave it a natural open-air feeling. To maintain the natural beauty of the place, no cars were permitted on the grounds. Access was achieved via the ferry or the people mover. A valet service was used that night to secure the cars at the dock, and take guests over on the ferry.

It was undoubtedly the place to be. The attendance of everybody who was anybody had been confirmed months prior. Hamilton International's marketing department had begun pushing the place during its final phase of construction, more than a year before it opened.

Its success was no doubt being solidified that night. It had appeared on the cover of Architectural Digest and the client waiting list was unbelievable. Aprielle's power and connections ensured that anything she got behind was a success. The opening was a mere formality, the final dotting of the i's and crossing of the t's.

"I'll see you in the morning, man," Mr. Hamilton said before heading off to the bar. He knew how to give her the right amount of support without interfering with her program.

"Where is Camille?" she asked.

"She's in the ladies room," I said.

"Darling, why don't you give Coleman a proper tour, and tell him all about the research plans. Excuse me a moment, gentlemen," she said, carefully masking from the mayor her displeasure with Camille's absence. Although not apparent to the mayor, Maximillian and I both knew that she was not happy. While she excused herself, I headed to the ladies room to try to warn Camille.

When I entered there were several women, including Camille, chatting and touching up their make-up at the vanity. Before I could get a word out, Aprielle burst in.

"Good evening, ladies. Are we enjoying ourselves this evening?" she said. The women respectfully returned the greeting. Camille rolled her eyes in the mirror.

"Would you ladies please excuse us? I need a private moment with my daughter-in-law." The women quickly gathered up their things.

"Tell the hostess outside the door that Mrs. Hamilton said to give each of you a Hamilton International Beauty Bag. It contains our new fragrance, which will be released next month, and a wonderful array of cosmetics. I think you will enjoy."

They thanked her and left. She discreetly checked the stalls, then situated herself alongside Camille at the vanity and powdered her face. As soon as the door was safely closed behind the women, she began. Neither woman interrupted their touch-up.

"Let me explain something to you, you ghetto wench. Part of being a good wife and hostess, is knowing when and when not to be in the ladies room—now is not the time! Maximillian is engaging the Mayor as we speak, someone who will be very instrumental in helping the Center get certain things done smoothly in this city, and where are you when you're needed for introductions? Nowhere to be found!"

"Apparently not—you found me." Camille said sarcastically. Aprielle let the remark slide.

"You should be out there next to your husband, smiling and looking stunning." She looked Camille up and down and said, "In your case, smiling." Camille calmly closed her purse and turned to face Aprielle.

"Maximillian doesn't need me standing next to him like some trained circus animal. He is more than capable of engaging the mayor and playing whatever particular brand of politics is necessary to ensure that things run smoothly for the Center, but something tells me that you've already made sure of that anyway, so are you finished? I need to run. We don't want to keep the mayor waiting, now do we? By the way, where's your husband?" Camille slung her purse over her shoulder, and turned to leave. Aprielle grabbed her by her arm.

"I certainly understand the importance of a woman's independence. However, that independence should never prevent her from exercising protocol and acting like a lady. Here's a solid piece of advice: don't draw a line in the sand with me—I'll cross it. I guarantee you."

Aprielle released Camille's arm and returned to applying her lipstick. Camille left without another word. "Gabrielle, this is precisely the kind of thing I tried to warn him about. A diction coach and a few charm classes are no substitute for proper breeding." She drew the strings on her bag and we left the bathroom.

We exited into a barrage of flashbulbs and commotion going on at the entrance. "Montgomery and Zoren Hamilton-Ross" was announced over the PA. When she saw

Montgomery through the crowd, smiling and indulging several autograph seekers, she said, "Who on earth among these guests would want his autograph? How dare he, after eight years, choose tonight to surface, playing 'Hollywood' and vilifying the Hamilton name by attaching some other man's name onto his." She bit hard into her lower lip, and took a deep breath. "If Camille wasn't enough, now I have this to contend with." She knew it wasn't the appropriate time or place to confront Montgomery. She eased the pressure on her lip, adjusted her dress and disappeared into the crowd. I headed over to say hello. I hadn't seen him in a month of Sundays. Montgomery caught a glimpse of Aprielle. He knew she'd seen him as well.

"Gabby, my favorite girl! How's life treating you?" he said, hugging me to tears. I pulled away, embarrassed that my emotions had betrayed me.

"Oh, cut that out! He said, "You're supposed to be happy to see your little Montgomery."

"I am happy. You have no idea how truly happy I am," I replied.

"I loved you first." Maximillian's voice came from behind Montgomery. He turned to find his reflection. Maximillian grabbed Montgomery, almost knocking him down. They still looked exactly alike, though Maximillian had put on a few pounds and Montgomery was wearing his head shaven. Maximillian's eyes welled up. "It is so damn good to see you," he said.

Maximillian was the emotional one. Montgomery was more like Aprielle when it came to emotions, although he'd die before admitting it.

"Don't you go getting all sappy on me," Montgomery said.

"I'm sorry man, for the way I acted. I never should have let so much time go by," Max said.

"That's behind us man," Montgomery said. Maximillian wiped his face, then suddenly burst out laughing, embarrassed about not being able to contain himself.

"It's just so damn good to see you, and what's up with this body, you must be hitting the iron everyday."

"Nah," Monte said smiling.

"Nah, my ass. Nigga you look like you been in the penitentiary," Maximillian said, poking Montgomery in his chest, squeezing his arms and pinching him on his butt.

"Will you cut that out, somebody might think you're trying to hit on me."

"So what," he replied.

"Yeah, right! You say that shit now, but you won't be so happy when you're in the check-out line and see '*Hamilton Brothers in Incestuous Love Affair*' splashed across the front of one of those tabloids."

"We'll just have to call in your spin doctors to handle it."

"I ain't got no damn spin doctors, you know I don't give a shit." Monte grabbed Maximillian's butt and started laughing.

It was great to see them laughing and enjoying each other's company. They had not seen each other since Montgomery moved to Europe. Maximillian refused to talk to Montgomery for years. He ignored all Montgomery's calls and letters. Interestingly, he had saved all of the letters, unopened.

Since Montgomery's return to the U.S., they had spoken regularly on the phone, but still hadn't seen each other. They both blamed it on their busy schedules, but I think they were afraid of what coming face to face again would be like after so long.

"So, where is this Zoren, who apparently has turned your world upside down?" Maximillian asked. Montgomery looked around. Zoren was no longer at his side.

"Some debutante probably has him hemmed up in a corner somewhere," Montgomery said. "He has yet to perfect that simple, two-letter word, No! You'll love him. He reminds me so much of Garrison." Suddenly, a look of horror came over Maximillian's face.

"Who?" Max said, seemingly puzzled.

"Forget that," Montgomery replied.

"Garrison? Who's that?" I thought to myself—primarily because there was something odd about Montgomery's response. The name didn't ring any bells with me.

Montgomery spotted Zoren a short distance away being chatted up by two beautiful women. "There he is, over there," he said. "What did I tell you? Let me go and rescue him." Montgomery headed over to where Zoren was standing.

He had told me that Zoren was quite the looker and drew women like a magnet. He'd said that wherever they went, women always found their way to Zoren. He knew it was entirely innocent and that Zoren was just being friendly, but he admitted that it often annoyed him, especially when women blatantly flirted with Zoren in front of him. From what I could see, tonight would be no exception. One of the women was clearly making her interest in Zoren known to anyone observing.

"Excuse me ladies, may I borrow my HUSBAND?" Montgomery said; loud enough that we could hear him clearly from where we were standing. The woman smiled, Montgomery smirked. Zoren politely excused himself. After which, Montgomery gave Zoren a piece of his mind.

"That shit is not cute."

"They were just being friendly, honey," Zoren replied.

"Too damn friendly."

"Come on, sweetheart, you know better."

"That is not the point and you know it. People don't respect our relationship as it is, and you ignoring their blatant disrespect only reinforces the shit. I'm tired of these bitches thinking that they can just push up on you, right in front of me."

"They weren't in front of you, honey."

"Zoren, don't split hairs with me. You know exactly what I mean. The bottom line is disrespect, and disrespect is disrespect whether I'm present or not. I suggest that you stop encouraging it. It's not like they don't know who we are."

Zoren put his arm around Montgomery and whispered something in his ear that made him smile. I smiled to myself thinking that Montgomery was more like his mother than he realized.

They made their way over to where Maximillian and I were waiting. Mr. Hamilton had joined us. Before anyone could say anything, Mr. Hamilton had snatched them both up in a big bear hug.

"Welcome home," he said, holding them so tight that if they had been smaller men he would have surely broken them in two.

Mr. H started to tear up. "Dad, don't start that," Montgomery said embarrassed. "Come on, let me go. You're wrinkling my suit."

Mr. H let them go. Zoren smiled politely.

"What are you crying for? You were just in Los Angeles. You act like you haven't seen us in years," Montgomery said.

"I know. It's just that I have never had you guys all together, in the same room, and I haven't seen you and your brother together in eight years. Do you realize it has been eight years?"

"My God, you've actually been counting!" Montgomery replied.

"Dad, look at these guys, they're huge," Maximillian said, awestruck by how big Montgomery and Zoren were.

Montgomery was considerably larger than he was when he left home. Neither of them was huge, but it was apparent that there were some well-developed bodies underneath their clothes, and when you hugged them, your suspicions were confirmed.

Zoren extended his hand to greet Maximillian, whom he had never officially met. "Hey, brother-in-law, I'm Zoren. It's a pleasure to finally meet you."

"Me too." Maximillian replied.

Maximillian gave Zoren an official *Cyrus Hamilton* bear hug welcome.

"Alright! Is everybody going to hug the man for an hour?" Montgomery said. "I can't even introduce him to everybody. Honey, this is Gabby. Gabby, this is Zoren."

Montgomery made the formal introduction between us. I stuck my hand out to greet him. "You might as well get your hug in too, Gabby," Montgomery teased.

I hugged him, making the Hamilton welcome complete.

"Have you seen your mother and Camille?" Mr. Hamilton asked Maximillian.

"Finally, I get to meet the infamous Hamilton women," Zoren said.

"Infamous indeed," I replied.

"Last time I saw them, they were heading toward the ladies room," Maximillian replied.

"So, they do go in pairs," Zoren joked.

"Not those two, trust me." Maximillian said, laughing.

Camille came up unnoticed and slipped her arms around Montgomery rubbing his chest. "Hey sexy," she said, "I've been looking all over for you. I hear you've been getting pretty chummy with the mayor."

"Excuse me!" Montgomery spun around to see who had their hands all over him.

"Meet my fun-loving wife, Camille," Maximillian said.

"Girrrl, you were 'bout to get…"

"Um-huh," Camille teased. "And who pray-tell is this hunkster?" she asked, referring to Zoren.

"That's *my* hunkster!" Montgomery said, teasing her back.

"I'm Zoren," he said, politely introducing himself.

"So, you're Zoren?" Camille said, flirting. Zoren extended his hand to greet Camille.

"Are you kidding me? Boy, you better get over here and press that hard body up against me, and show me some love."

Zoren stepped toward her to hug her. Camille was having a wail of a time kidding with both him and Montgomery. "Hmmm," she said, squeezing him as firmly as she could.

"Here we go," Maximillian sighed. "She's been bugging me for months about joining a gym, now you two show up making me look bad."

"You'd think a doctor would recognize the importance of exercise, wouldn't you?" she said.

"I exercise," Maximillian replied.

"And I'm the queen of Sheba."

"Where's my mother?" Maximillian asked Camille.

"I don't know."

"I thought she came to the ladies room to find you."

"She did, and that's exactly where I left her meddling ass."

"Not one of your favorite people, huh?" Monte said.

"Is she anybody's? Well, maybe you, Mr. H," she said smiling.

"You all cut that out," Mr. H said. "Maximillian, go have your mother paged." Maximillian went to the announcer's booth.

"So, tell me all about Los Angeles," Camille said, "I've always wanted to go there."

"You guys are welcome anytime," Zoren replied.

"Mrs. Hamilton, your presence is requested at the entrance." We heard the announcement being made as Maximillian returned.

"Honey, the guys and I were just talking about me going to L.A. to hang out with them," Camille said.

"What about me?"

"They said you can tag along." She gave him a wink.

"This place is some kind of amazing. You've done good, boy," Montgomery said, "A beautiful wife, an incredible facility, and a reputation that already precedes you."

"Look who's talking, you niggas all up in Hollywood on television and shit."

"Max, when you start talking like that? That shit's kinda sexy," Camille said.

"Oh, he's been perpetratin'. Trust, that nigga ain't ever been prim and proper. I know. I grew up with him," Monte joked.

"You boys better not let your mother hear you using that 'N' word," Mr. Hamilton interjected.

"What's she gonna do?" Monte said.

"Montgomery, don't start with your mother," Mr. Hamilton said.

"There you go. I already know how well meaning she is, so I don't need that lecture today. Okay?"

"You must have the patience of Job, young man, to share a life and a career with this one," Mr. Hamilton joked with Zoren.

"He's actually a sweetheart," Zoren replied, giving Monte a kiss.

"Oh, isn't that sweet. They're just too cute. Honey, how come you're not like that?" Camille said nudging Maximillian.

After several more pages from the announcer, Aprielle still had not returned. Mr. H went to have her paged again. Montgomery, tired of waiting, suggested that they find the bar. "I'll see mother later. I can see now that she's going to be acting like a bitch."

"Why would you say that about your mother?" Zoren asked surprised.

"Because I know my mother," he replied.

They all headed off to the bar, while I went to see if I could find her.

Aprielle finally surfaced. We had all gathered in the atrium for the ceremonial ribbon cutting when she appeared, virtually out of thin air, and joined Maximillian, Camille, Mr. Hamilton, and the mayor down front.

The mayor presented the Center with a commendation, which Maximillian accepted with a few remarks. He thanked his mother for her most extravagant and gracious gift and all her love and support. He also thanked Camille and his dad, and expressed how happy he was to have his brother

Montgomery and his brother-in-law Zoren present, sharing in the momentous occasion. Aprielle followed with a few closing remarks. She was poised in her remarks and did not let on in the least how discontented she was, but I knew. What looked like a proud, loving Hamilton clan to the public was anything but.

By the evening's end, tense was the only word to describe things. Following the ribbon cutting, Montgomery approached his mother to greet her and to introduce her to Zoren. She smiled and nodded, but didn't say anything. Mr. Hamilton announced that he wanted everyone to spend the night at the Hamilton house, so that they could have breakfast as a family the following morning. Montgomery immediately declined, stating that he and Zoren had already checked into a hotel downtown. After insistence from Maximillian and Camille, he finally conceded. Aprielle was adamant that if Montgomery and Zoren were going to stay that they had to sleep in separate rooms. That's when the argument erupted.

"Fuck that! We'll stay at the hotel like we planned," Montgomery said.

"That is probably best," Aprielle replied.

"May I see you in private?" Mr. H said to Aprielle.

"Not now, Hamilton," she replied.

"Then when?" he said, obviously angry.

"If this is about Montgomery and that boy sleeping together in my house, there is nothing to discuss. What he does in Los Angeles is his business, but I will not have it in my house," she said, then walked away. Mr. Hamilton went after her. Montgomery was livid. "I've had enough of her shit for one night," Montgomery said to Zoren. "I already let her obvious slight of you go without incident, but that's it. I'm not sleeping in separate beds for her or anybody else. I told you she was a bitch!"

"A royal bitch," Camille chimed in.

I went to see if I could talk to her. I found her and Mr. H on the dock. Mr. H looked very upset. He rarely got angry. He pretty much went along with her, but the one thing that he definitely had an opinion about was Maximillian and Montgomery.

He and Aprielle rarely saw eye to eye on matters related to them, but he never interfered in her relationship with either of them. He had his own relationship with each of the boys and was very active in both of their lives. Even after Monte had moved to Europe and vowed never to set foot in the States again, Mr. H made it his business to visit Montgomery four or five times a year, every year. He even took Jade with him at least two or three times a year.

"What is wrong with you, woman? Montgomery and Zoren have been together for years. Their relationship is no different than Maximillian and Camille's. What is the problem?" he said.

"Maximillian and Camille are married, and as much as I would prefer that that ghetto trash did not stay in our house either, she is Maximillian's wife and the mother of my grandchildren. Therefore, it is the proper thing to do."

"Proper, my ass. I am sick and tired of you treating him badly. You have not seen our son in eight years and this is the welcome you give him."

Mr. H was really hot. He never cursed, unless he was really, really mad.

"Cyrus, do not curse at me," she replied. Her tone was as even as it had been when she began. Her cool, detached way when you were angry at her only made you angrier.

"Aprielle, you cannot pretend like he doesn't exist. It's not going to make him go away. You need to let go of whatever it is that you're carrying about him. He's a good kid."

"A good kid? Hamilton, please. That is what is wrong with him now, you make excuses for everything he does. I guess in your opinion he's a good father too? I suspect all good fathers bounce around the globe while others raise their illegitimate children. Do not try to tell me about that boy. I birthed him. Montgomery is and always has been a selfish, spoiled, irresponsible little boy with crazy notions about how the world works, and as far as letting go, I did that a long time ago."

"Then why do you still try to control him? And frankly, Maximillian too."

"I do not try to control either of them. Maximillian just happens to realize, thank God, that I know a little bit about how things work, and he is willing to accept my advice and guidance. Not that he always follows it, evidenced by that wife he ended up with."

"Let's not discuss that," he said.

"You brought it up."

"Well, I'm dropping it."

"It's dropped. As far as I'm concerned, this whole conversation is dropped."

She turned and walked away. Mr. Hamilton returned to the bar where the boys and Camille were. "It's settled," he said, "everyone's staying at the house. I expect to see all of you at breakfast, nine o'clock sharp. Montgomery, you and Zoren can have you and your brother's old rooms. It's been a long night. I'm going home. You all make sure Rico or somebody drives you home. I mean it, you've all been drinking."

"I'll make sure of it," I told him. "What about Aprielle?" I asked.

"She knows her way home."

I could tell he was saddened by what had happened. He was so happy to have his boys reunited and all she cared about was the evening's fanfare, none of which he gave two hoots about.

I followed him back out to the dock. "Are you okay Mr. H?" I put my arm around his shoulder. "It's so silly, Gabby. All I want is to wake up and have breakfast in my house with my sons, like a family."

"She'll come around," I said.

"You know, I really couldn't care less," he said.

He turned and boarded the ferry. I went back inside to see if I could talk to her, but first I called Greta to tell her to have Maximillian and Camille's room turned down and the boys' old room prepared for Montgomery and Zoren. I knew what Mr. Hamilton was up to. He figured that if Montgomery and Zoren stayed in the boys' old suite, which were two rooms with a bathroom in the middle, Aprielle could presume that they slept in separate beds and feel like she'd won. Appearances were all she really cared about. He and I both had been around long enough to know that.

Chapter 17

"Good morning everyone," Camille said, as she dragged herself onto the patio looking a little worse for wear. Camille required at least an hour to get presentable. From the looks of things, she had overslept.

Greta had gotten the kids up early. They were out back playing when I came down. It was a beautiful day. The sun was peeking through the trees. Jade still didn't know that her father was in town. Maximillian got up to get Max Jr. and Madison so we could eat. A hair-raising scream, "D-A-D-D-Y!" came from the foyer. Jade ran into the dining area and hugged and kissed Montgomery and Zoren, who she referred to as D2. She had visited her dad and Zoren frequently with her grandfather since she was a little girl.

"Ooh Daddy, what a surprise. What are you doing here? I thought you were supposed to be on TV tonight?"

"It's taped in advance, honey. Come here and give Daddy a kiss."

Jade ran and jumped into her father's lap. "I love you, Daddy. It's so good to see you," she said before turning her attention to Zoren. "I know you brought me something D2! Where is it?"

"Up front on the table," he said.

"I knew it! I knew it!" She jumped down and ran into the other room.

Aprielle had not joined us yet. Mr. Hamilton instructed Greta to start serving as soon as Maximillian returned with the kids. "Come on and eat," I called to Jade.

"Say something, Aunt Gabby. Say something!" Zoren had brought Jade a video camera that she had thrust into my face begging me to say something.

"Come on, say something, Aunt Gabby, you're a movie star," she begged.

I laughed and said, "Something!"

"More than that! You're so silly, Aunt Gabby." She went around the table trying to get everybody to say something for the camera. Maximillian entered with Max Jr. and Madison.

"Look what I got Junior," she said.

"Ooh, let me see. Wait 'til after breakfast." Maximillian handed Madison to Camille and took his seat.

"Put that thing away and sit down, young lady," Mr. H said. "You've really started something, Zoren."

Greta served one of the best down-home breakfasts I'd had in a long time. We ate so much we were all ready to just stretch out in the middle of the floor. Aprielle never joined us. I wasn't surprised. I figured she was in the office working and probably waiting for me. The kids had run outside to play with Jade's new camera. I excused myself, so I could go get to work. "It's been an absolute pleasure to finally meet you, Zoren. I'm going to get to work. Be sure to stop in and say goodbye before you leave."

"Wait a minute, Gabby, I want you to hear this," Montgomery said. "I've given this a lot of thought, and I've decided that I'm going to take Jade back to California with me and Zoren. What I want to know is how do you think I should approach her about it?"

Mr. H spoke up immediately, "Why don't you start by asking her how she feels about it. After all, she's been with us all her life. This will be a major adjustment for her."

"When are you planning on leaving?" I asked.

"Actually, we were planning to leave today."

"Today? You can't just spring this on us and leave today," Mr. Hamilton was shocked. "You just got here. Why are you leaving so soon?"

"There's nothing here for me.

"Your family is here," Mr. H said.

"You know that I love you dad, but my life isn't here anymore, and little has changed around here since I left."

"I thought you two would at least come out to the house before you left," Camille interjected.

Montgomery decided he and Zoren would go out to Maximillian and Camille's house with them for a while, then he and Jade would go for a ride to discuss the possibility of her moving to California. If she wanted to go, he would take her, and if she didn't, he would wait and approach the subject again later.

Chapter 18

Aprielle and I were going over a licensing deal she was trying to close with an up-and-coming ball player, whom she wanted to market a new fragrance in his name and likeness. Jade tore into the office like a locomotive, "Grams, Grams!"

"What have I told you about that?" Aprielle scolded.

"I mean, Grandmother," Jade said.

"What is all the excitement about?" Aprielle asked.

"Daddy's..." She was so excited, her little legs were shaking and she could barely get a word out. Aprielle told her to come, sit down, and calm herself. She sat in her chair, a miniature version of Aprielle's high-back chair. Aprielle had had it made for her. She loved to sit in it and pretend like she was her grandmother, barking out orders to her imaginary employees.

"Now, tell me what all the excitement is about," Aprielle said, taking a yellow ribbon from her desk drawer and replacing the white one that was neatly wrapped and bowed around Jade's single ponytail. She apparently disagreed with Greta's choice to match the ribbon to Jade's blouse versus the butterfly patterns in her skirt.

"Daddy's taking me to California to live with him and Zoren," she said, barely able to sit still.

"Where in the world did you get such a ridiculous idea?"

"Daddy told me. He said that I could come and live with them in California."

"Your father should not be filling your head with such nonsense. You are not going to California, dear. Your father is too busy, and he and Zoren do not know the first thing about raising a child."

Jade's enthusiasm wasn't affected by Aprielle's disapproval.

"But I want to, and he said that I can."

"You are too young to know what you want, dear. Now go wash your hands." Aprielle nudged her from the chair.

"But I want to. I'm not too little. I'm almost ten," Jade protested.

"Do not sass me," Aprielle said.

Jade was quickly on her feet and headed for the door.

"Come back here, young lady," Aprielle summoned.

Jade came and stood on the side of the desk opposite Aprielle. She shifted her weight from one foot to the other as she looked off into space waiting for Aprielle to speak. "Stand up straight, Jade, and look at me." She looked directly at Aprielle. "I did not say that you are too little. I said, 'you are too young,' which means that you do not have enough life experience to make this kind of decision. Do you understand?" Jade nodded. "I said, do you understand?" Aprielle repeated.

"Yes," Jade replied.

"Very good. Now, run along. I'll talk to your father." Jade tore out of the office, with all traces of her previous excitement having vanished.

"Why is that boy filling her head with such ridiculousness?" she asked me. "He is an adult and I cannot do anything about where, how and with whom he chooses to live his life, but I will not allow him to drag Jade into his madness."

I couldn't have disagreed with her more, so I didn't say anything, which I had learned over the years was best.

"You obviously do not agree," she said, looking at me over the top of her reading glasses. She knew that silence was my way of disagreeing without confrontation. "Damn it, Gabrielle, so you are turning on me too," she said.

"No one is turning on you," I said, "I just happen to believe that children need their parents, that's all."

"What they need is good parents, which is exactly what she has," she replied.

"That can be very subjective. I think as long as a child isn't being harmed, they should be with their parents. Sometimes the pain of not being with their parents is far more damaging, and often not repairable."

"Jade is staying right here. She belongs in a stable environment."

I didn't say anything else. Montgomery and Jade entered the office. Montgomery was clearly upset and Jade was crying, holding her father around his waist. Aprielle motioned for Jade to come to her. She hesitated, then slowly made her way over to her grandmother.

"What is all this crying about?" Aprielle asked.

"I want to go with Daddy and you won't let me," she barely choked out through the sobbing.

"Your father and I need to talk. You go and find your grandfather and beat him at a game of checkers. Dry your eyes, now. What did I tell you?" Aprielle asked.

"Big girls don't cry," Jade said.

"Exactly! Now go find your grandfather," Aprielle said.

Jade looked to Montgomery for his reassurance that he was going to make everything okay. He nodded and winked at her. She left to find Mr. H. Once Jade was safely out of earshot, Aprielle lit into Montgomery, "See what you have done. What makes you think that you can just waltz in here and disrupt that child's life?"

"I'm not going to debate this with you. Jade and I had a long conversation about the pros and cons of her moving to California with Zoren and me. She feels comfortable with it and so do we."

"What does a nine year old know about pros and cons?" Aprielle asked.

"If I remember correctly, more than you think. Like I said, I'm not going to debate this with you. The question is not if she's going, it's how do we best make the transition."

"I am her legal guardian and I say she that is not going, and that is that."

"Oh, you think so?" he said.

"You know what, Montgomery, I am not interested in debating this with you either. So, let me make this clear, so that we can end this conversation. I am her legal guardian and I say she cannot go. Now, if you choose to leave here with her without my consent, I will, without hesitation, file kidnapping and child endangerment charges against you, period!" She turned her attention to me, "Gabrielle, where were we, before we got sidetracked with this nonsense?"

"I'll just sue you for custody," he said, "I'm stable and I can take care of her." He was shouting. She was completely unaffected by it.

"I do not think that you want to face me in court, Mister. We both know that your '*lifestyle*' will not play so well here in the Midwest."

"Are you threatening me?"

"You know me better than that."

"Then I guess you'll have to do what you have to do."

"I always do!" she replied.

With that, he left. I didn't see him the rest of the day. Aprielle and I went back to work. She was planning to make an offer first thing the next morning, and we still had several launch plans to review.

It was late when Montgomery returned. I was in the kitchen getting Aprielle and myself some tea. She'd decided we might as well burn the midnight oil to ensure that we had everything reviewed and approved on time. I asked him where he'd been. He said he'd been back out to Maximillian and Camille's house. He'd told Max what had happened and tried to see if he would talk to her on his behalf, but Max ended up telling him that he thought that Aprielle was right. He felt that since Jade had been with her and Mr. H her entire life, and with the kind of schedules he and Zoren had, it was probably best that she stayed here. Besides, the whole rest of the family was here. Montgomery said he wondered why he had even bothered: Maximillian always supported their mother's point of view. He said that Camille suggested that he just take her and face Aprielle in court, and that if she was any kind of mother or grandmother, she would refrain from taking them through that kind of drama. I assured him that would not be the case.

Monte decided to take Mr. H's advice, which was to have Jade spend the summer with him and Zoren, and see how things went. Later, they could consider moving her out there permanently. Meanwhile, Mr. H would be working on getting Aprielle to see that the move would be a good idea. I agreed. It wouldn't have been right to just take her away like that; after all, she had been with us for almost ten years and they loved her. I told him that I thought his father's plan sounded like the best approach for everyone involved. I also committed to doing whatever I could with whatever influence I had to get Aprielle to see that it would be good for Jade to be with him.

Later, Montgomery came to tell me that he and Zoren had decided to change their flight, and that they would be leaving on the red eye. I told him to be sure to stick his head in the office and say goodbye before he left. I was pretty sure we would still be up. He said okay, but I wasn't sure that he really would.

Around eleven o'clock, he and Zoren appeared in the doorway of the office. Montgomery came over and gave me a big hug and a kiss on the cheek. Zoren did the same to both Aprielle and me. Montgomery didn't hug or kiss his mother. He barely said goodbye, which I thought was an unnecessary slight. She didn't let it slide either. "Exactly how late do you have to stay up at night, to come up with ways to be nasty to me?" she asked.

"You know what? People like you get used to having things go your way, and after a while you begin to think that everything is supposed to. Life works out for you in ways that it doesn't for most people, but you need to understand that your power does not give you the right to just fuck over people!"

"Oh grow up," she replied, "people like you don't know a damn thing about people like me. I truly hope that the next time our paths cross, and never would be too soon for me, that you will have learned just a little bit about how the real world works. It was nice to meet you, Zoren. I wish you both a safe flight home."

I got up to see them to the door. "Gabrielle," she said, "they know their way out. We have a lot of work to do."

Chapter 19

By now, Madison was squirming around, whining for Camille, who had long since been removed from the main sanctuary.

The music quieted as Reverend Becker approached the podium. "Good afternoon. We've joined here today to celebrate the life of Dr. Maximillian P. Hamilton, one of our best and brightest." Reverend Becker's voice thundered through the sanctuary. He had an old Southern Baptist demeanor and the air of a modern day prophet. I glanced back at the funeral director, who shook his head in the negative—still no Montgomery.

"We all know that each of us must one day come this way, but that knowledge never readies us, never prepares us to say goodbye to those we love and…"

"There's a whole row of seats right down there," was shouted from the back of the church. I knew right away that it was Pebbles. She was incredibly late, trying to be seated.

"Those are reserved for the family, Madame," the usher responded.

"I am family."

"What is your name, Madame?"

"Pebbles."

"Excuse me?"

"Pebbles. Pebbles Sinclair."

The usher checked his guest list, while Pebbles arched her back and batted her eyes, to no avail. "I am very sorry Madame, but your name is not here. I am afraid you will have to find seating in the overflow area downstairs."

"That's ridiculous. Move out of my way." Pebbles pushed past the usher, but he managed to get in front of her, retaining her.

"Miss, you'll have to go to the overflow area downstairs."

"Move! I told you, I'm family," she insisted.

Pebbles surveyed the room anxiously looking for someone she recognized. She spotted Aprielle and broke past the usher running up the aisle toward where we were sitting. The usher caught her about midway and grabbed her arm. "Madame, you have to leave."

"Let me go," she screamed at the top of her lungs.

"Mrs. Hamilton, Mrs. Hamilton, tell this man I'm family."

Aprielle continued her forward gaze as if nothing was happening. I decided I had better put a stop to it before it went any farther. I motioned to the usher to let her go. She sauntered down to the pew directly behind us, which I was

saving for Montgomery, Zoren, and Jade, even though I was-
n't sure if they were coming.

Pebbles was inappropriately dressed, as usual, wearing a
black, front-zip cat suit and thigh-high patent leather boots.
She was showing more cleavage than should be legal. The
men ogled her, while the women shook their heads, some in
disgust, others in envy. She plopped down on the pew and
immediately tried to get Aprielle's attention.

"Pssst, Mrs. Hamilton, didn't you hear me calling you?"
Aprielle ignored her. "Mrs. Hamilton!" she repeated, raising
her voice above the original whisper. Aprielle glanced over
her shoulder and cut Pebbles a look that put an immediate
stop to her inquiry.

"Excuse me!" Pebbles mumbled under her breath as she
sat back in her seat.

"Are we all settled?" Reverend Becker said, speaking
directly to Pebbles.

He finished his welcome and began a Bible passage, divid-
ing his attention between the scripture and Pebbles. In the
middle of the scripture he abruptly stopped. His eyes were
fixed on the back of the church, as if Satan himself had just
walked in. I turned to find Montgomery standing in the
sanctuary entrance. The sight of him made everyone uncomfortable, evidenced by the incredible amount of fidgeting, as
people tried to find comfort by adjusting themselves in their
seats. Most people there were aware that Maximillian was a
twin. Due to Montgomery's television popularity,
Maximillian found himself constantly explaining that he was

not the guy on TV, and fighting off aggressive autograph seekers. Some folks simply wouldn't believe him and insisted on an autograph. He'd often oblige, just so he could get on about his business. Despite this knowledge, the impact of Montgomery standing in the entrance was chilling. I was equally taken aback, as we watched the dead come to life. Mr. H instantly broke down. "Parents aren't supposed to bury their children. That's not how it's supposed to be," he said, sobbing. Aprielle patted him on his leg, more to quiet than to comfort him. Mr. H rose.

"Cyrus, where are you going?" Aprielle said.

"I'm going to wrap my arms around my boy."

"Not now, Cyrus," she said, pulling him back to his seat, "there will be plenty of time for that. Haven't we had enough outbursts?" He sat back down, but he kept his eyes fixed on Montgomery.

"Where is your handkerchief?" she asked. She motioned for the nurse; Pebbles handed him some Kleenex from her bosom.

"Here, Mr. Hamilton, I have plenty," she said smiling. Aprielle cut her another look, this one more venomous than the first.

The usher escorted Montgomery, Zoren, Jade, and a well-dressed young man that I didn't recognize, to where Maximillian lay. Zoren held on to Montgomery as he stood at the casket for what seemed like an eternity, staring at his mirror image and softly stroking Maximillian's hands. He adjusted his tie and hanky, then he leaned over and kissed him on the cheek and mouthed the words "I loved you first."

I could feel myself being summoned to his side. I wanted to go and throw my arms around him and reassure him that everything was going to be okay. I remained seated, though. I could see that Zoren had everything under control. Realizing it was time, Zoren placed his palm lightly on Montgomery's lower back and sympathetically encouraged him to move along. Jade approached the casket, clasped her hands together in a prayer-like formation and bowed, Japanese style, in honor of her uncle. Her handsome escort repeated the gesture.

As they passed me to take their seats on the pew behind us, I could see just how stunning and womanly Jade had become and how handsome her young escort was. He had full almond shaped lips, his best feature, and clear Hershey smooth skin that illuminated against his all black ensemble. His shoulders were broad, his posture erect, and his crown of neatly aligned plats gave him the air of a young African prince. Jade had her hair pulled back in a chignon. She was wearing a simple black dress and matching jacket. Her Hamilton strength and sophistication permeated. Our little Jade—all grown up and wearing make-up—brought me to tears. I searched my purse for a tissue. Pebbles handed me one over my shoulder. "Will you knock it off with the Kleenex," I snapped.

"I was just trying to help."

"First you come in here late, being extremely disruptive I might add, and ever since you've been here, you've been talking and passing out Kleenex like you're the nurse. If you really want to be helpful, sit back and be quiet!" She seemed stunned by my remarks. I thanked her for the Kleenex and refocused my attention on Montgomery, who instead of taking his seat with Zoren and Jade, went directly to the platform.

In order to make it convenient for those giving remarks, there were three podiums on the platform, one to the far left, the far right and one in the center. Montgomery joined Rev. Becker at the center podium.

"Greetings Brother Hamilton." Reverend Becker stumbled over his words, obviously surprised, as was I that Montgomery was at the podium. Montgomery whispered something to him and as the Reverend sat down, Montgomery began.

Chapter 20

"This is especially difficult for me. How does one say goodbye to a part of himself? How does one live half in this world and half in another? How do I reconcile the resentment that I feel toward many of you who are in some way responsible for my pain?" Montgomery said removing his sunglasses. The melancholy in his eyes gave emphasis to the deep pain we could hear in his voice.

"How do I continue to feel love for you when you have destroyed a part of me? These are the things I will have to grapple with."

Because I was down front, I couldn't see most of the guests in attendance, but sadness and bewilderment was upon the faces of those I could see. I wasn't sure what Montgomery was getting at, but I knew it wouldn't be long before he made it clear to all of us.

"Last night, after years of utter silence, I received a call from my mother. A call that turned out to be the most callous of gestures. At a time when I needed her love and support most, though I wasn't foolish enough to believe such a thing possible, she called to offer me some self-righteous, judgement-laced invitation to return to her inhospitable home. She said, and I quote, 'In this time of grief and loss, you should take the opportunity to atone and rejoin the company of those who truly love you.' Needless to say, her comments only reinforced my sense of alienation and exacerbated my feelings of pain and sadness for my brother, and the hell he must have suffered through at the hands of such a heartless, narrow woman."

Aprielle's gasp set off a chain reaction that reverberated throughout the room. Rico somehow managed to interrupt her rise to her feet. I reluctantly looked over at her. She was beside herself. "Gabrielle, what is he doing up there?" she whispered to me from beneath her hat. "I don't know," I said, shrugging my shoulders. I wasn't sure that he'd even come. I certainly didn't know why he was up at the podium or what he hoped to bring about, but I was sure that we were all about to find out.

Camille, who had returned to her seat and her senses, as much as that was possible for Camille, was looking at me in her ever-colorful way as if to say, "girrrrl, this shit is about to get good." She was clearly taking pleasure in this unfolding drama, particularly the discomfort and embarrassment that it was causing Aprielle.

I passed Madison to her. She was thrilled to see her mother again. Max Jr., on the other hand, seemed none the wiser. He was completely engrossed in Montgomery.

"As I contemplated what I would say in tribute to my brother," Montgomery continued, "I decided to begin by listing his accomplishments, his adventures, his hobbies, his dreams, and his secrets. As I went through the lists trying to decide what to say, it struck me that most of you probably didn't really know my brother. My initial thought was to leave it that way. You had certainly had the opportunity, but in all probability hadn't provided him the safety to fully show himself to you. I thought, why should I be the one to let you in on the fullness of a spirit you didn't care to really know? Then I decided, maybe I should be the one, because to not share, would be to spare you from the guilt that you should forever carry."

"All right, that's it! That is ENOUGH!" Aprielle was on her feet. Rico couldn't stop her this time. "Montgomery P. Hamilton, you come down from there this instant. You are not on the program."

"It's Hamilton-Ross, Mother. Come now, you know the importance of a name."

Camille laughed out loud. She was happy that someone else was putting Aprielle in her place for a change. Aprielle glared at Camille, to which she paid absolutely no attention.

"Sit down, Mother. I trust that you'll want to spare yourself and the family any additional embarrassment."

Rico whispered something to Aprielle, who after a brief protest took her seat. Mr. H buried his face in his hands. He was happy to see Montgomery, but not happy about the inevitable battle brewing between the two people he loved.

"Where was I? Oh, yes!" He continued, "I actually had not planned to be here today. I knew that, for the sake of appearances, the truth would not be spoken here. I knew that even the unusual circumstances of my brother's death would not be enough to spur the truth. More importantly, I knew that one more sterilized, politically correct memorial service was more than I could stomach. So, I had decided to stay home, that is until I read this article in *USA Today*. After reading it, I realized that I had to be here. I had to be the one to bring out the truth, for Max Jr., Madison, and—"

"Hi Uncle Monte!" Madison blurted out, waving enthusiastically to Montgomery. "He is not calling you, he is simply referring to you. Now be still," Camille told her.

"Hi, Sweetie," Montgomery said, smiling warmly at Madison.

"See, yes he was, Mommy," Madison said.

"Shhhh, be still, Madison."

Camille quieted Madison and Montgomery went on. "The article I'm referring to is a reprint that has appeared in several leading newspapers around the world. When I read the headline, I nearly fell right out of my chair. It read, 'Study Finds Heterosexuality Not Natural, Not Normal'."

Suddenly, people began murmuring, but I couldn't make out what was being said.

"Let me repeat that. 'Study Finds Heterosexuality Not Natural, Not Normal.' I don't know about you, but the headline alone thrills me."

Several people laughed, Camille, of course, among them. Aprielle inhaled deeply and shook her head in disgust. Rico put his face in his hands. The laughter, however, lightened the tension in the room. It was like we were being held hostage.

"The article explains something that is of major importance. It outlines, backed by much research data, how the heterosexual/homosexual division of modern society is nothing more than a superficial social construct, and therefore deconstructable. It clarifies how the supreme arrogance of the heterosexualization of society has permitted us to view this heterosexual/homosexual binary as rooted in biology, nature, or evolution. When I read this, all I could think was that finally, the unquestioned, axiomatic assumption of heterosexuality is being questioned both publicly and internationally.

"I realize that most of you don't think so, but I know a few of you here know that a hallelujah is in order."

Montgomery shouted, jumped up and down, and spun around like he was imbued with the Holy Ghost. A few heads in the crowd nodded in support.

"Oh, by the way," he said, "you can put your programs away. We'll be deviating from the printed program, but please take it home and read it at your leisure. I'm sure it contains all the good stuff you expect."

Folks laughed—more than had laughed earlier, myself included. Aprielle was clearly not amused. I have to admit that a large part of my laughter was to camouflage my confusion. I consider myself to be an intelligent woman, but what Montgomery had said about a heterosexual/homosexual binary had flown right over my head.

"Despite appearances, today is a very good day, and for those of you who don't believe in coincidences, you'll agree that our being here today, some of the most prominent and influential people in business, medicine, politics, and the media, is no accident. Because if what this study has found is true, we are about to embark upon a radically free and different future that will hopefully eliminate our need to gather under these tragic circumstances ever again."

His humor and mockery gave way to complete seriousness.

"I think that we can all agree that children have a natural need to look into their parents' faces and see joy and approval reflected there. I think that we can also agree that most children pretty much want to be the source of happiness and satisfaction for their mothers and fathers. Are we in agreement so far?"

Heads reluctantly bobbed in the affirmative.

"Well, some children quickly realize that if they reveal who they are, not only will they no longer see that look of affirmation, they will become a source of pain and disappointment to their parents. They promptly figure out that in order to continue to be a source of happiness to their parents, to be affirmed, and to be accepted, they will have to pretend. My brother, God rest his soul, did exactly that: he pretended.

"Maximillian achieved your acceptance at the expense of his integrity. He exchanged the trappings of success for the turmoil of incongruity, and the pain of living separated from his soul in a world of fear and denial."

Curiosity transfixed the room. People whispered back and forth in confusion, trying to discern what in the world Montgomery was talking about…and what any of it had to do with the news article and Maximillian's death.

"What my brother didn't understand when he made that choice, and Lord knows neither did I—at least not in psychological terms—was the trauma he would eventually experience as a result of failing to come to terms with his identity. My brother lived a lifetime in a state of conflict and contradiction, pretending to be something he was not—heterosexual!"

The place went into an uproar. "Oh my God!" someone shouted from across the room. Pebbles fell out in the aisle. Reporters immediately got on their cell phones to their editors. Aprielle was back on her feet yelling at Montgomery to come down from the podium. Everyone else was gasping, gagging, acknowledging, or debating the truth of what they had just heard. Camille looked at me with "I told you so" written all over her face. I turned away, stunned by what I had heard and horrified that Camille was taking such pleasure in watching the family being publicly humiliated by one of its own.

"Put those FUCKIN' phones away!" Montgomery shouted. "You all are missing the whole point. It is precisely because of assholes like you that we're here. I didn't come here to give you fodder for gossip. I came here to enlighten you."

"Are you satisfied?" An incensed Aprielle was heading to the front of the church. "Is this why you came here, to tear us down? To sully your brother's reputation, something he cared about?" Rico caught her before she made it to Montgomery. All pretense was now gone. "Let me go, Rico!" she said through clenched teeth.

"Mother, please, save it, and would somebody get that chile up off the floor."

The usher helped Pebbles up, and with the assistance of two nurses, Rico escorted Aprielle out of the sanctuary. I could not believe what was happening. People seemed afraid to move. It was clearly an uncomfortable situation, but no one appeared to know quite what to do. I slid over to comfort Mr. H, who had not said one word. Unbelievably, Montgomery continued.

"My brother's choice to live a heterosexual lie on the surface seemed easy enough. It was definitely supported by everything around him: popular music, television, newspapers, magazines, billboards, movies, and even casual conversations. Wanting and needing your approval so much, he created a mask, a pseudo-self, so that he could fit in with all of you. If he had had the balls to say 'fuck you,' maybe he'd still be here."

Reverend Becker immediately went over to Montgomery. He spoke to Montgomery for a few minutes. It had to be about the profanity he was recklessly using. After Montgomery and Reverend Becker finished their sidebar, Reverend Becker returned to his seat and Montgomery went on.

"Ladies and gentlemen, Reverend Becker, forgive me. I didn't mean any disrespect. It's just that when it all fell apart for Max, I'm the one he called in the middle of the night, hysterical, talking about how embarrassed he was with who he had become. How he had spent his whole life sidestepping the truth, hedging and outright lying to himself and everyone around him, lest he jeopardize his place in the family and his social circle. We cried together on the phone like little children. I knew then that the chicken had come home to roost and there was nothing I could do."

Montgomery broke down. Zoren went to his side.

"Come on, let's sit down," Zoren said.

"No, I'm not finished," he replied, "I have to say what I came to say."

Without protest, Zoren took the empty seat next to Reverend Becker. "I'm right here if you need me," he said. He passed Montgomery a handkerchief. Montgomery wiped his face and continued.

"As I listened to Max sob, I became weighted with anger. I was angry about society's ridiculous demands that seem to crush so many spirits. I was angry with our parents for not protecting him. I was angry with him for the choices he had made, and the pain he was experiencing because of them. I was even angry with myself, for not outing him a long time ago. I had abandoned him years before, and for that I was both angry and sorry, but in truth, it was all I could do at the time to save myself."

Montgomery paused a moment to collect himself.

"I've seen too many times the disillusionment and loss that so many suffer as a result of attempting to assimilate. I realized a long time ago that trying to become what you are not has a price. Unfortunately, my brother had to learn this after acquiring so much to lose.

"I encouraged him to get professional help. I even invited him to fly out that night to spend some time with Zoren and me. I knew I was reaching, but I thought that maybe being around us, witnessing two men loving each other, contributing to the community and raising a daughter like any other family, might help him on his journey. Sadly, evidenced by the fact that we are here today, that was not the case.

"There's no doubt that Max always knew that he was sexually attracted to men. His struggle and confusion was never about the truth of his desires, but how to reconcile them with the world around him.

"Max and I both became aware of our sexual inclinations in junior high school. At least, that's when we named it and spoke it. We spent many nights up late discussing our desires between ourselves. I never felt any shame. There was something deep within me that always provided me comfort.

"It wasn't until we got to high school that I became aware of the shame Max carried. One day we were sharing secrets like always, and I told him that I thought that Terry, this guy on the high school basketball team, liked me. I told him how at every game, without fail, Terry would search me out in the crowd and smile at me. Max didn't believe me, so in order to prove it to him, at the next game we sat on the visiting team's side. When the players came out, we could see Terry combing the crowd looking for me. He looked disappointed that he didn't see me. Finally, when the players came out of their huddle, Terry looked up and saw me sitting directly across from him, on the visitor's side. He lit up like the First Family's Christmas tree. Max realized that I was telling the truth. I told him that I was going to ask Terry out, since I didn't think he had the guts to ask me. Max begged me not to and made me promise not to let anyone know that I liked boys. He was concerned that if people found out that they might think that he liked boys too. I promised him that I would not.

"As time went on, we both secretly fooled around with boys that we knew wouldn't say anything. Terry and I got together a couple of times before he graduated. I'm sure his NBA fame would compel him to deny it.

"Midway through our junior year, Max suddenly stopped going out with me. When I questioned him about his sudden about-face, he said that he wanted to run for Senior Class President and felt that having a girlfriend would make that easier, which didn't make sense to me, because we went to an all-boys school.

"In retrospect, I realize it was at that time that Max began to actively create his heterosexual persona.

"When we got to undergraduate, I broke our little pact and started openly dating guys. I occasionally went out with women, which explains my lovely daughter. Interestingly, they knew that I was into men, but it didn't stop 'em. I think it was a bigger challenge for them, not to mention that sensitive, gay guys had a reputation for knowing how to treat a girl like a lady.

"In college, Max exclusively dated women and never said anything about my antics. We had solidly established our separate identities by then. We had different friends and completely different personalities. He, the conservative one, and me, well, let's just say I'm the one who ran around campus in outrageous T-shirts with slogans like, *Smart Men Don't Become Doctors, They Marry 'em.* Max had me convinced that his earlier experiences had been nothing more than a phase...until he came home with Garrison, this extremely handsome and charming Jamaican. I clocked it right away.

"In the following months he and Garrison were inseparable, and the ladies were no longer a staple around the apartment. They dated for two and a half years, and even talked about futures together. As graduation approached, Max started acting strange. I chalked it up to nerves about going to medical school. He eventually told me that although he didn't want to, he had to break things off with Garrison. Although he loved him, he couldn't see how they could have a real future together. 'How is a prominent doctor going to show up at important functions and family dinners with a man?' he said. 'Shit, just show up!' I said. I begged him not to break up with Garrison. Hell, I'd been actively dating men since we arrived on campus and I had not found what they had. I told him not to let fear make him do something that he would later regret. That advice fell on deaf ears. After two and a half years, he dropped Garrison without explanation.

"Max went on like Garrison had never existed, refusing any communication with him. Garrison tried everything. He sent flowers and waited outside Max's classes. I remember him sitting outside our apartment, in the rain, for hours, waiting for Max to come home. I felt terrible. Garrison was a really nice guy and the way Max treated him was selfish, cruel and undeserving.

"At some point, I became sick of it and decided to meet with Garrison to try to shed some light on the situation the best I could. I explained to him that Max was really scared and concerned about what the family would say, which Garrison found surprising since I was so out there.

"When Max found out that I had met with Garrison, he was so mad. We had a huge fight. He accused me of betraying him. He even said that I was probably trying to get Garrison for myself, which was absolutely not true, but when he called me a sick faggot, that's when we came to blows. When it was all said and done, we weren't speaking and Garrison had been dismissed as a perverse phase. He never breathed another word about Garrison, nor did I. To endure the pain that he had to have felt when he walked away from Garrison, and to act as if nothing happened, was an indicator to me even then that Max was in deep trouble.

"I decided I needed to distance myself. I was deeply hurt by the nasty things that he had said to me, and I couldn't believe that he was capable of being that insensitive and seemingly not care. It was difficult for me to buy his rationale that being straight was the key to success. Our mother was much too powerful for that to matter. I didn't believe it was about success at all; it was about not upsetting mommy.

"Max had surmised that in order to truly be accepted by our mother, he had to maintain a heterosexual image. He had witnessed her disapproval of me. He'd heard her endless expressions of rejection, couched in semi-loving terms, when she'd say things like 'I do want you to be happy, you're a Hamilton'…as if that meant anything on its face. Max caught, as I, the distinct difference in the tone of her voice when she talked about what he was doing versus what I was doing. To this day, she takes great pride in talking about her son, the doctor, his children, and even the daughter-in-law she doesn't even like. I'm sure when the topic of me, the other son, arises, she becomes evasive or has some little pat response like, 'Montgomery's fine; we're both so busy we rarely talk,' which is more convenient than true.

"I would venture to say that my mother has probably never spoken a prideful word about my and Zoren's relationship or the work that we do. Sadly, her love has always been conditional: get good grades, graduate from this school, marry that person, make me look good, then I'll love you. Basically, we could please ourselves and lose her, or please her and lose ourselves. I opted for the former, he the latter. The difference in our choices was always the strain on Max's and my otherwise-wonderful relationship.

"I remember when I ditched law school and left the States, Max declared me dead. It hurt, but I soon understood his anger. He had always lived vicariously through me. My leaving removed his outlet, and with me—the perpetual scapegoat—no longer around, it was difficult for him to hold on to the illusion that our mother really loved him, an illusion I'd let go of a long time before.

"When I was perceived to be heterosexual, my family and so-called friends accepted me as normal. Once I began to show myself as a lover of men, things changed. My desires made me a social outcast, and attempts began being made to take my entitlements as a perceived heterosexual away. If you understand the dynamics of male privilege, then you understand the dynamics of heterosexual privilege; they're cut from the same cloth.

"Coming to terms with this realization early on enabled me to move on. As a result, I am able to stand before you today: one of the happiest, wealthiest, most well-respected men in this country. If I'm not living the American dream, I don't what it is. And what makes it all the sweeter is the love and support I have from the most incredible man I know."

He looked back and winked at Zoren.

"You go boy!" Pebbles shouted out, evoking laughter from the majority of the room. Even Montgomery had to laugh. Pebbles indeed had a way of bringing humor to an otherwise humorless situation. I couldn't bring myself to laugh, but I did smile. Montgomery winked at Pebbles and continued.

"Ladies and gentlemen, at the bottom of my sadness and impatience is my longtime understanding that the hetero-sexual/homosexual divide—two discrete, essentially differ-ent types of people—is not nature's doing, but society's. We're all a mixture of impulses and practices and what someone does with a willing partner is of no real social or cosmic significance.

"Just as many of you were ready to tolerate homosexual-ity, provided that your own heterosexuality remained undis-turbed, here we go pushing the envelope. You see, to present heterosexuality as an historical social convention, rather than as a natural and eternal given, challenges all your tradi-tional assumptions about heterosexuality, and brings into question the legitimacy of your heterosexual emotions, behaviors, relationships, and identities."

He laughed.

"I'm sorry, this really amuses me, because even as I say it, I know that the average person cannot conceive of a society where heterosexuality would not order all things. You see, for you to regard yourselves as normal, natural, and greater, someone else has got to be regarded as unnatural, abnormal, and lesser, which when you really think about it is ridiculous and points to what I believe is the catalyst for all the hatred that we experience. Sadly, God and the Good Book get the role of justifier.

"I beg you not to take my word on any of this. I encourage you to get the article and examine its content.

"Before I close, I'd like to ask my dad to join me. Come up here, Dad."

Mr. H joined Montgomery at the podium and greeted him with an embrace. Without letting go, Montgomery reached into his jacket pocket and pulled out a tattered piece of paper.

"When I was fourteen years old my father gave this to me."

He held the paper up. Mr. H looked surprised.

"I'd like to share it with you today," he said, then began reading from the paper.

> *When you get what you want in your struggle for self*
> *And the world makes you king for a day*
> *Just go to a mirror and look at yourself*
> *And see what that man has to say*
> *For it isn't your father, or mother or mate*
> *Whose judgement upon you must pass*
> *The one whose verdict counts most in your life*
> *Is the one staring back from the glass*
> *Some people may think you're a straight shootin' chum*
> *And call you a wonderful guy.*
> *But the man in the glass knows you're only a bum*
> *If you can't look him straight in the eye*
> *He's the one to please, never mind all the rest*

For he's with you clear to the end.
And you know you've passed your most dangerous test
If the man in the glass is your friend
You may fool the whole world down the pathway of
years
And get pats on your back as you pass
But your final reward will be heartache and tears
If you've cheated the man in the glass.

Montgomery turned to his father, beaming with pride and said, "Thank you, Dad. Thank you for your love, your support and your wisdom, and although he's not here, I know that Max thanks you too. You personify the true meaning of love. Only a man with a higher understanding could love the likes of me and my mother so deeply and unconditionally."

Montgomery brushed away his tears. "In closing," he said, "I hope that each of you understand that the pursuit of happiness and the glory of the human experience in this twenty-first century is up to each of us. Be careful not to diminish another's light, and whatever you do, refuse to participate in the destruction of another's spirit. Let my brother's demise be the example of how not to treat your fellow man."

With that, Montgomery took Zoren's hand and walked down from the stage, up the aisle, and out of the church. No one moved. We all sat there wondering what to do next.

Chapter 21

The room was still as we sat there in silence. There wasn't a dry eye in the house. I began to applaud, slowly at first, increasing the rhythm as others joined me in acknowledging these boys' pain, and apologizing for any role I may have played in it.

Mr. Hamilton took his seat and a bewildered Reverend Becker returned to the podium. "I believe everything has been said, Amen?"

"Amen!" we responded in unison.

"At this time we will proceed to Memorial Park Cemetery for the entombment," he continued. "Due to the large number of people here, please remain in your cars and allow the parking attendants to assist you in joining the processional. The dove release will be done at the cemetery."

Silence was replaced with chatter about what we had just experienced. It certainly was not the service anyone had expected.

Chapter 22

When we exited the church, Rico had already joined Aprielle in the back of the second family car. Montgomery was in the third car with his legs hanging out, smoking a cigarette. Max Jr. asked Camille if he could ride with Montgomery. She agreed. She and Madison were escorted to the family car directly behind the hearse. Jade and her friend Michael, at Mr. H's request, accompanied him to the second car where Aprielle and Rico were. Klein, Fitzgerald, their wives, and the Hamilton International and Center staff were seated in the additional family cars. I was doing a final check of the family cars to make sure that everyone was accounted for, when I noticed that Pebbles had weaseled her way into the car with Montgomery. I didn't say anything.

The attendant announced that we were ready to leave and began closing the doors from the rear of the procession, as the motorcycle escorts got into position. On my way to get myself seated in the car with Aprielle, a bald, handsome gentleman approached me, asking the where-abouts of Montgomery. I took him to the car where Montgomery was. "I just wanted to thank you for that in there," he said, squatting down beside the car. Montgomery looked confused by the man's statement.

"You don't recognize me, do you?" he said.

"I'm afraid I don't," Montgomery replied, seemingly searching his mind for clues.

"It's me, Garrison!"

Montgomery leapt from the car, grabbing the guy and hugging him with such force that he almost knocked him to the ground. Immediately, I knew he was the man that Montgomery had alleged to be Maximillian's college admirer.

"Oh shit! I can't believe this…I was just talking about…well you know that. I wondered what had happened…Man, I wouldn't have recognized you in a million…What happened to your hair?" Montgomery babbled on in excitement.

The two of them laughed, hugged and looked each other over for all the obvious and not so obvious changes that had occurred in their appearances since they had last seen each other.

"Come on, get in, you can ride with us," Montgomery said.

"Thanks, but I'm not going to the cemetery. I just wanted to say hello, and thank you for reminding me of how beautiful my time with Maxi really was. The pain of the break-up left me so numb that I had actually forgotten," Garrison said.

I couldn't imagine Maximillian allowing himself to be referred to as Maxi. It seemed that I was learning more and more about a man I thought I already knew.

"Where are my manners?" Montgomery said, realizing that he had completely forgotten about the rest of us. "Garrison, this is Gabby, my surrogate mother."

I blushed with pride and embarrassment. I had no idea that he felt that way about me. It felt good. It was in fact the best feeling I had had all week.

"In here," he said pointed into the car, "is my honey, Zoren, Maxi's son Max Jr., and Ms. Sinclair, his office manager. Everybody, this is Garrison Cooper, a very old and dear friend."

Zoren and the others leaned forward to acknowledged Garrison. While we were exchanging greetings, an attendant came over and informed us that we needed to take our seats, because the procession was about to leave.

Garrison decided to go to the cemetery after all. I told him that I would make sure that his car was brought to the repast, if he wanted to ride with Montgomery.

While I was instructing one of the attendants to make sure that Garrison's car got brought to the repast, the procession began pulling off. Fortunately, Montgomery wouldn't let his driver leave without me. I climbed in with them. The attendant guaranteed that he would switch me to the car with Aprielle if and when the procession stopped.

Montgomery assured Garrison that his car would be fine. "They work for my mother, and no one fucks with her, except me of course!"

We laughed. When an assertion is that truthful, all you can do is laugh.

Pebbles, who had obviously not been paying attention during the service, was sitting so close to Garrison that I wasn't sure that the poor man could breathe. She had her breast pressed shamelessly against him, and she kept reaching across him, fumbling with things on the bar.

"So, what are you doing these days?" Montgomery asked Garrison.

"I'm a partner in EWF."

"E-World Financial?"

"That's me! My partner and I merged two smaller companies to form EWF about seven years ago," Garrison replied.

"So, you're living in Japan?"

"Not anymore. Everything's so global now. There are offices in Tokyo, Switzerland, and New York, but we live in New York."

"We?" Montgomery said, surprised, implying that there was more to "we" than Garrison was telling.

"My business partner is also my spouse," Garrison replied.

"Does this spouse have a name?" Montgomery kidded.

"His name is David Yakatomi."

"Yakatomi! Get outta here. I see you quit messin' with these crazy ass Americans too, huh?"

"I can't say that it was premeditated."

"Shit, it was for me—fully. They got way too many issues for me, especially the brothers."

"OK!" Pebbles interjected. Then in Japanese, she asked Garrison how he liked Tokyo, to which he replied.

"Tokyo was great, I lived there for a little over five years. Do you speak the language fluently?"

"Yes, among others," she said, flirting.

"Really?"

"I'm fluent in French, Spanish, German, Russian, Japanese and, of course, English. My Masters is in International Business."

"Very impressive, Ms. Sinclair."

"Please, call me Pebbles."

"With those language skills, Ms. Pebbles, you would be a definite asset to EWF."

"Is that an offer?" she said in perfect French. I didn't know what was worse, her shameless attempts at impressing him with her foreign language skills, or the tongues that her body was speaking. I thought to myself, what part of spouse and David Yakatomi didn't she understand?

"Here's my card. If you're ever looking to make a move, call me."

Garrison gave her one of his business cards.

"What happened to your dreads, man?" Montgomery said, mainly to take back the conversation.

"Wow, I cut those off right after Maxi and I broke up. I was pretty distressed, and at the time didn't want anything that reminded me of him."

"I hope you didn't cut off everything that reminded you of him?" Montgomery joked.

"Montgomery!" I interjected, reminding him that there was a child in the car.

Suddenly we stopped, the door opened, and one of the attendants stuck his head in to tell me that a train was holding us up, so if I wanted to change cars, now was the time.

The attendant escorted me to the other car, where the mood was quite different.

Rico was knocked out, snoring like a broken bass drum. Mr. H, in another world, had his head resting against the car's interior, quiet as a church mouse. Aprielle was busy cross-examining Jade about her friend.

She was right in the middle of asking, "Young man, what are your exact intentions toward my granddaughter?" She didn't interrupt her interrogation to ask where I had been.

"Grams, don't do that!" Jade said, embarrassed by the question.

"I have to make sure that this young man is more than attractive," she said. "Your father has evidently lost his mind, so I undoubtedly cannot trust his judgement."

"Please don't start talking about Daddy," Jade said.

"I will be more than happy to refrain from talking about him, but you must admit that that little performance at the church…"

"Aprielle, I thought you just said that you weren't going to talk about him?" Mr. H interjected.

"I'm not. I'm just saying…"

"Which means that you're talking about him," he replied.

"I'm outta here!" Jade said, reaching for both Michael's hand and the door handle.

"Don't act ugly, dear," Aprielle replied.

"Can we just change the subject?" Jade said.

"Of course. What would you like to talk about?" Aprielle conceded.

"Anything, except Daddy and Mike's family tree."

"Well, I must say that your hair is lovely, dear, wearing it up works beautifully with the neckline of that blouse, and the suit is stunning. Who is it, dear?"

"*Dolce Gabbana*," Jade replied.

"Oh, they are so trendy, dear! I suggest that you stick with the classics."

"A second ago it was stunning, now it's too trendy. There's no winning with you." Jade replied.

"I was not speaking of that particular suit, dear, but you have to be incredibly careful with trendy designers, they simply aren't consistent."

"Whatever!"

"I thought we were not going to fight, dear?" Aprielle said.

"You're the one! Why can't you just compliment me without a critique? Is that too much to ask?"

"I wasn't criticizing you, dear. I was trying to be helpful. I realize that you do not have a woman around to teach you certain things. For example, your makeup, although very lovely, it is a tad heavy for daytime. Wouldn't you agree, Gabrielle?"

Jade rolled her eyes at Aprielle so hard, I thought that they were going to roll out of her head.

Although the make-up was a bit heavy, I was not about to agree and have her feel like I had teamed up against her. I was convinced that if one more word was said about what she was wearing or doing, she was going to leap from the moving car.

I knew Aprielle was really trying. Their relationship was very important to her, evidenced by the fact that it had managed to survive despite the tumultuous one between her and Montgomery. She adored Jade and wasn't trying to alienate or embarrass her, but she sure wasn't doing a good job of avoiding doing just that.

"So, are you coming to intern with us this summer?" I asked Jade, attempting to change the subject to avert the fight that neither of them wanted.

"No, Gabby. Mike and I…"

"Why can't you say Michael and Gabrielle? His name is Michael isn't it? Did everything I taught you those first ten years of your life go right out the window?" Aprielle said, shaking her head in disgust. "Parents go through a significant amount of thought in selecting their children's names, only to have them shortened and chopped all up. It is entirely nonsensical."

"What! Why are you trippin'? Grams, it's just too formal," Jade replied.

"It is not too formal, and please stop calling me that!" she said, irritated.

"I always call you Grams," Jade laughed.

"And I don't like it!"

I had to commend Jade for trying to keep it light. Aprielle had undoubtedly embarrassed her in front of her friend, and continued to challenge and criticize everything that she said. Most teenagers would not have been so tolerant.

"And what is this talk about not coming to intern this summer?" Aprielle asked, now categorically upset.

"I'll be in London working on my CD this summer," Jade replied.

"What CD?" Aprielle asked. She thought about it for a moment, then it registered what Jade meant. "Singing!" she shrieked in horror.

"Yes, singing!" Jade replied.

"Oh my God! Not you too. Honey, you have everything going for you. You are beautiful and smart. You have resources, dear. Singing is for people who don't have anything else." She turned her attention to Jade's friend, Michael. "Do not tell me that you sing, too?"

"No, Ma'am," he replied.

"Thank goodness. Maybe you can talk some sense into her. What are your career plans, son?"

"When I finish school…"

"Oh good, college!" Aprielle interrupted; relieved that at least one of them was on a track she approved of.

I knew from the way Michael looked at Jade that that relief would be short-lived. He would surely let the wind out of her sails with his next statement. Jade decided, however, that she'd do the dirty work, "He's NOT going to college. He produces hip-hop artists, which I am one of. He is very talented and good at what he does, and YES, I love him. Hopefully, that answers ALL your questions, GRANDMOTHER!"

"Cyrus, do you hear this?" Aprielle said, nudging Mr. H.

"Why don't you leave those kids alone," Mr. H replied.

"You are as juvenile as they are. This is her legacy I'm talking about. I did not build Hamilton International for a stranger to run."

She was beside herself, that she wasn't getting any support from Mr. H or me.

She woke up Rico, "Rico!"

Just then, the car stopped.

"Whew, thank God we're here," Jade said.

Before the attendant could get the door opened fully, Jade bolted from the car, dragging Michael with her. He did manage to squeak out, "Nice to meet you."

Chapter 23

We were all gathered quietly at the Hamilton mausoleum in the small private cemetery, where not too long before blacks weren't allowed, no matter how much money they had.

The Hamilton mausoleum was among the largest, made of Italian marble and surrounded by a half-acre of well-manicured landscaping. The family's name was engraved on the front, and an eternal flame fixture was at the entrance—a well-defined final statement of the family's importance to the community.

None of us would have ever thought that Maximillian would be the first Hamilton to take up residence in the marble palace.

After all the drama at the church, Aprielle thought it was best that the graveside remarks be kept short.

Reverend Becker said a prayer, the casket was slid into the wall, the flame was lit and the mourners were quietly directed back to their cars, with directions to the repast.

I noticed Montgomery and Garrison sitting together on one of the marble benches outside the mausoleum. They looked good together, which suggested to me that Garrison and Maximillian had made a fine looking couple.

I thought of the journal, wondering if there was any mention of Mr. Garrison Cooper in it.

Camille informed us that the interment would be her last Hamilton appearance. She'd decided that she and the children weren't going to the repast. She said that they had been through enough. Although the gathering wasn't going to take place anywhere near the room where the bodies had actually been found, she said that she was not taking her kids anywhere near where their father had been killed. That re-ignited the previous argument she and Aprielle had had about the responsibilities of the repast.

Camille had refused to have the repast at her house. She didn't want to put up with a bunch of folks she didn't know in and out of her house. Aprielle contended that as his wife it was her responsibility to host the repast at their home. Camille's refusal, in Aprielle's opinion, further accentuated just how little she loved and respected Maximillian.

Aprielle told her that the Hamilton house was out, she was done bailing her out of one faux pas after another. If she didn't want the family and friends of the man who had provided her with a life that she would have only dreamed of without him, then that was fine with her. The repast could be at the Center. At least she knew that the people there cared about him.

None of the immediate family ended up going to the repast. Montgomery said that he and Zoren were heading back. They took Garrison by the Center to pick up his car, which I had had taken there. Jade and Michael opted to go visit some of Jade's friends in Toronto, which she hadn't seen in a while. Mr. Hamilton was so emotionally distressed that he was relieved when Aprielle said she wasn't going. I myself was glad she didn't want to go. I had had more than enough—the detectives, the crowd, reporters, not to mention her and Camille. All I wanted to do was relax in a hot bath.

Chapter 24

When we got to the house, I asked Aprielle if she needed anything. She said she wanted to be left alone. That was all I needed to hear. I went to my room to relax.

I could not get Montgomery's comments at the service out of my mind, and meeting Garrison Cooper in the flesh made it especially surreal. I wondered if I had indeed been looking the other way all those years. Camille and Montgomery were aware of things that the rest of us seemingly didn't have a clue about, which had me feeling a little betrayed.

I kicked off my pumps, started a bath, and curled up on the chair and waited for the tub to fill. The journal, which I had never gotten around to telling Montgomery about, was lying on my desk. The temptation to read it was at its peak. Suddenly, I could hear my grandmother: *"Honey, there's at least three sides to every story, and the truth ain't in none of 'em."* What the heck, I thought, Camille was probably right, Max wouldn't care if I read it. By doing so, I could at least get his side of the story. Maybe there was something there that could help me help Aprielle understand. I wasn't so much worried about her personal embarrassment—she'd weather that—but watching Maximillian's reputation (something she had worked so tirelessly to build) be destroyed was enough to shatter her. She loved both those boys, and though she couldn't relate to Montgomery, she still loved him deeply.

As I sat there debating whether to read the journal, without warning a sweet familiar sound brought to my face a smile as wide as a pelican's wingspan. It was triggered by a splash outside my window...a sound I had not heard since Maximillian's death. Boy, how I missed that sound! I hurried to the window to watch him, like I'd done so many times before.

Chapter 25

I have no idea what got into me, but when Rico finished his laps I was standing there in my stocking feet, holding a towel. He was startled when he came up and found me there.

"What's wrong?" he asked.

"Nothing," I replied, handing him the towel to dry off.

"Is Mrs. H okay?"

"Everyone's fine!" Suddenly, I began to cry.

"What's wrong?"

"I'm feeling all these things that I can't sort out."

"It's been a rough week for all of us. Don't worry, things will settle down."

He pulled me close to him and moved my hair from my face. I was shivering like crazy. The temperature had to be in the low-thirties.

"Let's go inside, you're freezing," he said. He scooped me up in his arms. The cold air against his warm body created an aura around him. I felt my nipples hardening against his chest. I prayed that he'd hurry and get us into the house before he noticed.

When we got to my quarters, he put me down on the sofa. I became nervous with him that close to me, half-dressed.

"Can I get you a cup of that tea you like?" he asked.

"Actually, I'd prefer a cup of your famous cocoa."

"I didn't know it was famous," he replied.

"To some of us it is," I said, smiling like a love-struck schoolgirl.

Rico left to get the cocoa.

"What are you doing?" I thought. Rico always was available if I needed help with a stuck jar lid, a last minute errand, a cup of tea, anything, but it was always professional. This time there was something in the way he asked me if he could get me a cup of tea, not to mention the way I responded, that felt far from professional.

I was getting up to go get my slippers when I remembered the bath water. I ran into the bathroom, praying that I had shut it off. Fortunately, I had.

"Gabby!" he called from the other room.

"I'm in here," I said. "That was fast."

"Greta already had a pot on when I got down there."

"So, you cheated," I joked.

"If it'll make you feel better, I'll go pour this out and make it myself."

"You'd do that?" I asked.

"Of course I would."

He put the tray down on the table and sat in the chair next to the bed. "This is very nice," he said, admiring the room.

"You've never been up here?" I said, knowing full well that he had never been in my sleeping area.

"I brought you some butter cookies. I thought they might cheer you up," he said.

"How sweet," I replied.

Our hands brushed slightly as we both reached for our cocoas at the same time. I lowered my eyes and smiled. "Excuse me," he said.

"No excuses necessary." I replied.

I couldn't believe I had said that. I was downright flirting with him. "So what did you think of Montgomery's—dare I say—eulogy?" I asked, trying to change the subject. It was all I could think of to shift the focus from the unprofessional thoughts that were on my mind.

"It's funny that you should ask me about that," he said. "Though I thought that Montgomery definitely could have found a better way to make his point, there was something that he said that I haven't been able to get it off of my mind."

"Oh? What's that?"

"Remember when he said that straight men created faggots so that they could sleep with them without becoming faggots themselves? Then he gave the example of how athletes treated guys like him in college—having sex with 'em in private, then berating them in public?"

"Yes, I do remember that."

"He was so right."

"How would you know?" I asked. My heart sunk. I put my cup down on the tray to keep from dropping it. Why had he told me this? Was he speaking from experience? No wonder he'd never approached me. What I had been reading as sexual tension between us was obviously anything but. "Are you gay, too?" Before I knew it, I just blurted out.

"Oh no, Gabby. I'm not…I'm sorry…I shouldn't have…"

"I mean, you can tell me if you are," I said. "I don't think there is anything wrong with being gay." I was trying to be supportive, but I'm sure he could see the disappointment on my face. I wanted him to reassure me. I needed to hang onto the fantasy that he really wanted me, but respected me too much to make a move. More importantly, I needed having secretly wanted him for all of these years to mean that I actually had a chance of having him, even if I never did.

"I assure you, Gabby, that I am not gay."

"Have you ever had sex with a man? I asked. "I mean, Montgomery did make it sound like it's some kind of college rite of passage, or something."

He laughed, which was good because it definitely lightened the mood.

"Why did you even tell me that?" I asked him.

"At the moment, I'm really not sure, but it wasn't confessional in nature, I assure you. There actually was a point. I think what I was trying to say is that when Montgomery was talking about the athlete situation, it occurred to me that at some level that's really how I saw him, and that really bothered me."

"What?!"

"Don't get me wrong," he said. "I love Montgomery to death and I would hurt somebody over him, but I have to admit that I've always separated Monte—the kid that I watched grow up—from Montgomery the gay guy. And like those athletes, having been one myself and having even participated in the berating—not the sex, just the berating—part of me is repulsed by him. But hearing him speak today really helped me to better understand exactly who he is, what he's gone through and what it means for him to love another man."

All suspicions of him possibly being gay were instantly dissolved. I was actually moved by what he had said. I picked up my cup and further contemplated what he had just said. Montgomery had said so many things that I think everyone there must have been experiencing some sort of introspection. The thing that I was left with was the painful realization that, like Maximillian, I wasn't living the life I had imagined for myself.

I had always dreamed of being an artist. Actually, the idea of owning my own little gallery had been a big part of that dream. I guess I had become too caught up in Aprielle's world to realize it. Somehow, a part-time temporary position had turned into the rest of my life. I shared my thoughts with Rico, to which he replied, "It's never too late."

"That's sweet," I said, "but running off to paint at fifty-something doesn't seem very sensible."

"Have you ever painted anything?" he asked.

I pointed to the portrait hanging over my bed. It was one of my very first paintings in school. I couldn't remember the last time I had sat down and put brush to canvas. I wasn't even sure I still could.

"You did that?" he said, seemingly surprise. "You're good. I mean very good."

"Thank you," I said, "but that was a long time ago."

He got up to take a closer look. He admired every detail with absolute appreciation expressed in his eyes.

All of my years of desire for him began to burn inside me. I got up and went to the bathroom.

"You know Gabby, you really are very good," he shouted over the running water.

"Flattery will get you everywhere," I shouted back.

"No really, I know you are not going to believe this, but I was a child art prodigy, and I know good work when I see it."

"Yeah, you're right. I don't believe you," I said.

"Ask Mrs. H, she'll tell you."

"How would she know?"

He didn't say anything. I finished collecting myself and returned to the room. He wasn't there.

"Is this your mother?" His voice came from the other room. I went to the doorway. He was admiring the photos on my desk.

"Sort of," I replied.

"Am I being too personal?" he asked apologetically.

"It's not that," I said. "She's my grandmother. My mother died during childbirth. My grandparents raised me, but they're both dead now. Though they took great care of me, I've always longed for my real mother.

"I know exactly how you feel," he said.

"Really?" I replied thinking he was about to tell me a little bit about where he was from.

"I'll tell you about that another time. Right now I want to do something that I have wanted to do for a long time."

He reached over and kissed me gently on my lips, then paused and waited for my permission to continue. I melted into his arms, giving him full consent to proceed. He pulled me to him and kissed me again, deeper and more passionately than the first. The powerful attraction between us had finally shattered all barriers.

He stared into my eyes, which must have been twinkling like Christmas lights. I could already feel moistness between my thighs.

He cupped my breast, then gently stroked the curves of my body. My breath quickened when his hand came to rest between my thighs. My pulse raced through my body. I wanted him, but in the back of my mind, I was afraid that this moment of passion might result in the destruction of a lifelong friendship.

He hesitated, sensing my retreat. I glanced over his shoulder into the wardrobe mirror. We looked good together. His body was as tight as any twenty-year-old was, and thanks to the time that I'd spent exercising, I looked pretty good myself.

I decided to take the chance. I circled one of his nipples with my finger, which he took as his cue to continue.

He slid my blouse slowly off my shoulders, showering my neck and shoulders with light kisses. He picked me up and carried me into my sleeping area and began to undress me. His confidence made it easy for me to surrender.

He quickly had me down to my bra and panties, the set Camille gave me for my birthday. I had told her at the time that a Wonder Bra was the last thing I needed at my age. Suddenly, I was silently thanking her.

"Garters?" he said.

"You disapprove?" I managed through broken breaths.

"Definitely not," he replied. "I think they're the sexiest undergarment a woman can wear."

With that, he patiently removed each of my stockings.

The towel around his waist had risen like fresh baked bread. He turned me around, pressing his firm chest against my back, and gently cupped my breasts from behind, continuing to deliver an avalanche of kisses to my neck and shoulders.

His hands slowly moved from my breasts, along my abdomen, down to my inner thighs. He picked me up and stretched me out across the bed, peeled away his towel and trunks, and slid onto the bed alongside me. A lump as large as a Ping-Pong ball rose in my throat.

He was perfect. I laid there taking him in, recording every inch of him in my memory. He was uncircumcised, and had salt and pepper pubic hair that trailed up to his navel. I thought of how handsome a subject he would be to paint.

He massaged my body with soft delicate strokes. His touch was like velvet. There was nothing rushed about him. "How come you never approached me before?" I managed between the kisses.

"Probably for the same reasons you never did," he said, then slid between my legs.

I reached down for his ampleness. His long, hard flesh jerked spastically at my touch. He sighed, and his whole body grew rigid as I stroked him.

He gently moved my hand away. "Patience," he said, in a whisper.

I was thinking, "The lone star of my fantasies is lying between my legs—patience is something I simply don't have the luxury of." I wanted him. I wanted him in my most private place, and I wanted him right then.

He elevated himself above me on his elbows, his lower body still pressing against me. There was a pause that seemed to last forever, while he stared into my eyes. "I want to make love to you, Gabby," he said gutturally. "If you have doubts, act on them now."

"I have no doubts, Rico. Only regrets that we've waited so long."

I let out a suffocating cry when his long fingers probed and found the sensitive folds of my moist, burning readiness. My legs separated, my back arched involuntarily, I grabbed his butt, rough with impatience and pulled him closer. "Take me!" I screamed, then I screamed it again, "take me!" And he did.

Chapter 26

Iawoke to Rico's scent on my pillow, accompanied by a long stemmed red rose and a note. My heart sank. I presumed the rose was intended to make the disappointment a little easier for me to bear...the pain I was certain to feel after reading excuse after excuse as to why he would not be going to Italy with me.

We'd stayed up all night making love and planning our future together. I was going to resign my position with Aprielle, he was going to take a leave of absence, and we were going to spend a few months in Europe painting and taking in the old country. When we returned, he would help me open the gallery I had always wanted, and once he had helped Aprielle find a replacement for him, he too would resign and we would...

Oh, what did it matter? It was obviously just talk. I should have known better. That's just how men are: they tell you anything during the throws of passion.

After a few minutes of harsh, reprimanding internal dialogue, I decided not to let my inner-talk get the best of me and opened the letter.

Good Morning, Sunshine!

Please forgive me for not being there to personally greet you with a warm hug and delicate kiss. When I got up for my swim, you were resting so peacefully I didn't dare wake you, although I did miss you watching me from the window. I think this is probably the first morning in a long time that you weren't there.

I found Mrs. H leaving this morning, heading up to Marquette to get away for a few days. I thought it best that I take her. She's been through a lot and I didn't feel comfortable letting her go on the road by herself.

I thought a lot about our discussion last night, and unfortunately, I've had to reconsider. It has absolutely nothing to do with you, Gabby. There is nothing I'd enjoy more than spending the rest of my life with you.

I have felt you watch me from your window each morning for many years, and knowing that you'd be there to watch was my motivation to show up each day. The torch you've carried for me all these years, I've also carried for you…since the first day I saw you, when you showed up at the house in Palmer Woods, frozen half to death. I knew then that we'd be together. I had no idea it would take this long, but you know what they say about those who wait.

Remember yesterday, when I told you that I knew exactly how you felt about longing for your mother? I told you that I would tell you about it some other time. Well, I never knew my mother either. I was given away when I was a baby.

My mother's parents wouldn't allow her to keep me. She was sixteen years old at the time, visiting relatives here in America for the summer, when she got pregnant by my father, whom I've never met either.

When her family found out that she was pregnant, they told her that she could not return to their home with her nigger baby. They made her remain here through her pregnancy, then forced her to return home without me once I was born.

I ended up in foster care, moved from family to family. During the second year with my fourth foster family, an elegant lady in a big car pulled up in front of our house, in Denver. I was about fourteen years old. She got out and came to the door. She was too perfect-looking to be a social worker and she definitely didn't look like anybody my foster parents would know.

I fantasized that she was my mother and had come for me.

She met privately with my foster parents first, then with me. She told me that she was taking me to New York, where I would live with her, go to high school and work for her company. I didn't want to go. I had just made new friends, which was always hard, because I looked so different. My foster parents strongly encouraged me to take the opportunity. I felt like they were throwing me out.

The next thing I knew, my stuff was packed (all of which she later discarded), and I was off to New York with a woman whose name I didn't even know. When we got into the car, she introduced herself, then asked me if Rico was short for Ricardo or something more formal, and I said, "No". She simply smiled.

She took me to New York, and did everything she promised. She took care of me, gave me a job, and put me through college.

On graduation day she threw me a big graduation party. That night after the festivities, she handed me an envelope postmarked March 10, 1943. It was addressed to an April Louise Johnson. When I saw it I got nervous. "What is this?" I asked her. "Read it," she said.

It was a letter from our father—yes, Aprielle is my half-sister.

Our father had written her and told her about his relationship with my mother. He asked her to promise to find and look after me if anything ever happened to him, because she was all the family I had.

She said that she never responded to the letter, nor had she seen or spoken to our father, for years prior to or since receiving it. However, she'd made a promise to herself that if she ever became aware of his demise, she would try to find me and see after me.

Gabby, as much as I'd love to join you on what I am sure would be a rewarding and wonderful journey, I can't leave her now, not when she suffered so much loss. With you leaving and Camille and the kids moving to the West Coast, Mr. H and I are all she has left. Who knows where I'd be if it hadn't been for her? She needs me to return a favor. I truly hope that you'll understand.

Please don't let this change your plans. It's time for you to go, to follow your dream.

I just hope that whenever you hear the splash of water or take pleasure in a good cup of cocoa, you'll think of me.

Always, Rico

It wasn't nearly as bad as I had suspected, but all of the courage I had had when I decided to resign and take a chance on myself was now gone. Knowing that Rico was going with me made it seem doable. Now that he wasn't, I didn't know if I could go through with it. Then I heard it, one of my grandmother's quips: *"Nothing beats a failure but a try."*

I pulled myself together, deciding that I owed it to myself to at least try. I sat down to organize a plan.

While rummaging around in the closet for my luggage, I found a stack of my old paintings. I pulled them out and looked through them. There was one of Jade as a baby, Maximillian and Montgomery when they were about three or four years old, some landscapes, a few still lifes, and one of a young Rico emerging from the pool, dated 1968.

I couldn't believe that so much time had passed. I decided to leave it for him. I attached a little note that read, "*My Dearest Rico, you are as virile as the canvas illustrates. Love always, Gabby.*"

Looking through my work reinforced my decision to leave. I sat down to pen a very difficult resignation letter to Aprielle. I would definitely miss her. I'd practically grown up with her myself.

After I sorted my things into those I would travel with now and those I would send for later, I packed the former and called the travel agent and booked a flight to Rome.

I called a taxi, took my luggage down to the foyer, and went to say goodbye to Mr. H and Greta.

I had just missed Mr. H. Greta said that he had just left for the golf course to try to relieve some of his stress. I was truly sorry that I had missed him.

I gave Greta the portrait of Rico and asked her to take it to his quarters. I went back upstairs for a final look to make sure that I hadn't forgotten anything.

Maximillian's journal was on the floor beside the bed. My initial thought was to take it with me and read it on the plane. I picked it up and sat on the edge of the bed. I ran my fingers over the imprint of his name. I could smell his scent on it. I skimmed through it and stopped on one of the last entries.

My happiness is supposed to be mine, but it's not. I know why

I'm so despairing lately. It's because I want to be loved by everybody, and I've finally come to realize that that's a human impossibility. I could be the most delectable, the most delicious, the most wondrous peach in the world, but there are people who don't care for peaches—they prefer bananas. So, I became a banana to please the banana lover, only to find that the next one preferred apples. What started out as a wondrous peach, wound up as a messy fruit salad…

"I'll be right there!" I yelled down to Greta, who was letting me know that my taxi had arrived.

I went to my desk and addressed a big, padded envelope to Montgomery. I put the journal in it and dropped it in the outgoing mail basket on my way out to the taxi.

Maximillian had chosen to show me the man that he wanted me to know, and that was good enough for me.

Chapter 27

We'd put at least sixty miles behind us before a single word was spoken. I was trying to give Mrs. H some peace and quiet, and I was having trouble taking my mind off of Gabby. A part of me really wanted to go with her.

I had the radio tuned to my favorite jazz station. The music that typically soothed me was completely ineffective. The question that had continued to trouble me ever since finding Maximillian's body was gnawing at me again.

It had played over and over in my head consistently since that day. Whatever it was that had prevented me from asking her sooner had subsided. "How did you know to go to there that day?" I asked her.

She didn't respond. Her eyes were fixed on the road. I knew she had heard me, so I waited. After a few minutes of silence and her repeated motions to smooth the nonexistent wrinkles from her skirt, she replied, "I arranged it."

"Arranged what?" I asked.

"The meeting," she said, pausing briefly before continuing. "Paul was not supposed to be there. Maximillian called me, very upset. A mother does everything she can to stop her child from hurting."

I was having a hard time making heads or tails of what she was saying. The latter statement seemed more for her than for me. She went on talking, partly to herself and partly to me.

"Maximillian told me that he wanted out of his marriage and needed my help. I thought that was a good thing. It's no secret that I never wanted him to marry that trash, but when he told me that he wanted out of the marriage so that he could pursue men, I lost it."

My eyes left the road just long enough to almost hit the car in front of us.

"I couldn't bless that, now could I?" she said.

"No, of course not," I replied. I didn't know what else to say. I didn't necessarily agree with her, but I wasn't sure that I had really comprehended what she said.

"Maximillian was spotted at an adult bookstore several years ago. The person who saw him there contacted me in an attempt to extort money. I told him that everyone knew that Montgomery was gay and that he had been disowned by the family long ago, so he could sell his story to anybody who was stupid enough to buy it, but I was not interested."

"Montgomery? I thought you said it was Maximillian?"

"It was, but he didn't know the difference."

I turned the radio down, hoping it would help me get a clearer understanding of what she was trying to tell me.

She asked me to turn it back up, because she liked the song that was playing. I did. She continued.

"'The feelings are back, Mother. I need your help,' was what he said, Rico. 'They're back, Mother.'

"I told him that he was too close to having everything that we'd worked so hard for to go and mess things up. The work that he was doing had the potential to transform the medical community. He said that he hated himself, that he was a farce, a fake, and a liar. 'SHUT UP! Shut up this instant,' I told him. 'You are a Hamilton! That's what you are. Do you understand me?'

"I made it clear to him that I did not want to hear another word about any of it. If it was an occasional boy that he needed, we could arrange that. It's done all the time. There was no need to go upsetting the apple cart after all this time.

"He became enraged, which frightened me. He started shouting and crying, 'Mother, you don't understand. I want love. I want to be loved. I want what I had with Garrison.' That was that boy Montgomery saw fit to tell the entire world about yesterday."

I couldn't believe it. She had known all along. At the church she had seemed as surprised as anybody had. As it all began to register, I became sick to my stomach.

"I tried to get him to understand that he was not built like Montgomery. Montgomery came here equipped to live that life. Maximillian didn't have that—that's why I had to protect him."

Her eyes welled up. "I told him, they would eat him alive. If he thought that the politics were thick, he hadn't seen anything. Introducing gayness into it would be a death wish. He said he didn't care. He didn't want it anymore.

"It wasn't about what he wanted, Rico. If he had come to me with this prior to marrying that girl, I could have arranged something suitable. Things like this are successfully dealt with all the time. It would have been very simple. I could have found him a nice young lady from a proper family, perhaps even with similar inclinations. He would have been free to have a male friend on the side, and everyone would have been clear about their roles and responsibilities. I even suggested that maybe Camille, with the proper prodding, would agree to a similar arrangement. They seemed to be spending quite a bit of time apart anyway. He said, 'No way. I married her for love, and I could never ask her to do that.'

"Rico, I tried. I did all that I could do. I attempted to help him. Everything I suggested, he rejected. I cautioned him that there was much more than his feelings to be considered. He needed to remember the big picture.

"Finally, he said that he was willing to let the chips fall where they may, which illustrated to me that he had no loyalty to this family, or respect for what I had built for him. I could not allow him to destroy everything I'd built, and I certainly could not permit him to leave a veil of disgrace for his children to have to live through. Disgrace is especially hard to undo. I had a legacy to protect."

I pulled off at the next rest stop. I was fearful that if I wasn't at a standstill when I asked her my next question, her response might make me kill us both.

I turned the radio off. I swallowed hard. I turned to her and said, "Are you trying to tell me that YOU killed Maximillian?"

She slowly turned in my direction, taking her eyes off the road for the first time in the entire conversation. She looked me square in my eyes. If looks could kill, I would have been casualty number three.

THE END—For Now!

What Becomes

Of A Legacy

A peak at the follow up to
How To Ruin The Perfect Child

And The Winner Is

Montgomery came back from the men's room just as the nominations were being announced.

The presenters came forward to present the award. "The nominees for Best Director are James Cameron for *Surrender*; Blaine Teamer for *Pandora's Trunk*; Montgomery Hamilton-Ross for *How to Ruin the Perfect Child*; and Michael Mann for *Day Trader*; and the Oscar goes to Montgomery Hamilton-Ross for *How to Ruin the Perfect Child*."

When Montgomery heard his name, he turned and looked at Zoren, who said, "They called your name. You've won. Get up there!"

The critics had pegged Montgomery to win it. The movie had done well at the box office, taking in over 500 million dollars, and was being hailed as the most moving and provocative film since *Ordinary People*.

The Academy being the Academy, everyone had figured that the honor would go to Michael Mann, since it was

Montgomery's first picture and Michael had struck out in his last attempt, when *The Insider* failed to beat Sam Mendes' *American Beauty*.

When the reality that he had won sunk in, Montgomery made his way to the stage. He never actually thought he would win. On their way to the ceremony he and Zoren had joked about award shows being a lot like cruising. You spent an enormous amount of time and energy in anticipation of the ultimate experience, then it was over in an instant, and it wasn't until after it was over that you knew whether you were a winner or a loser.

Montgomery looked a little nervous at the podium. "Unlike most of the nominees this evening, I have never dreamed or imagined being here, which makes standing here all the more thrilling. I'm here because of a set of very unusual circumstances.

"A lot of people think that you have to go out and turn the world upside down. In my experience, just being true to myself has always somehow managed to turn the world on its head."

Supporters laughed, while Zoren, Gabby, and Jade applauded.

"I guess I'd better thank some folks. I definitely didn't do this all by myself, and I owe a great deal of thanks to a lot of wonderful and talented people. Of course, I want to thank the Academy, and each of you who helped to make *How to Ruin the Perfect Child* bigger than any of us could have ever imagined. I want to thank the producers, Stephanie Harris,

Dana Hugle, Francesca Miller and Deborah Morton, four courageous women who believed in the project, and were not afraid of the subject matter.

"I have to thank the cast and crew, especially Terrance Howard and Lynn Whitfield for delivering performances that every actor from this point forward will undoubtedly be measured by. Those of you who know my mother know Lynn nailed her.

"I want to thank my son, Onyx, for keeping me laughing through the making of this picture. Without that, I don't know if I could have gotten through it. I thank my lovely daughter, Jade, for making me so proud. You all go out and get her new CD called *Jade: More Precious than Stone.* That title couldn't be truer.

"I want to thank my Uncle Rico and Aunt Gabby. Gabby, thanks for everything, especially for seeing to it that the words got into my hands.

"I have to thank two of the most important people in my life, who aren't able to physically be here tonight, but I know they're here spiritually. I feel them guiding and pushing me every day: my father, the late Cyrus Hamilton, a man who never let me down, and my brother, the late Maximillian P. Hamilton, without whose words none of this would have been possible. I miss you both dearly.

"I want to acknowledge my brother's widow Camille, and their children Madison and Maximillian Jr. We did it, guys!"

He held the trophy up in the air toward them.

"Oh, I hear that music. I'd better hurry up. Please, bear with me—I only have one more person to thank.

"My mother said, at my brother's and my birth, that someday we would take our place in America's who's who of black firsts. She said it was our destiny, and I guess she was right. It is with great pride that my accomplishment this evening allows me to join such a unique and prestigious group of African Americans, my brother among them, who have inspired and changed the course of this great country.

"As notable an honor as it is to be the first African American to win an Oscar for Best Director, it is an even greater honor for me to be the first openly gay African American to do it.

"You've heard the old saying, 'Behind every great man there is a woman'. Well, behind some great men there is a man, and I would be remiss if I didn't acknowledge and publicly share this honor with my partner, my friend, my man, Zoren Hamilton-Ross. Honey, would you please come up here and take your place behind me!"

The crowd erupted with laughter and applause.

"Just kidding."

Zoren passed Onyx to Jade. "Bring Onyx with you," Montgomery said. "I want both of you up here beside me." Zoren scooped Onyx up in his arms and joined Montgomery at the podium. The three of them looked dashing. Onyx was especially adorable in his Armani tuxedo.

Montgomery was so full of joy, he was moved to tears. "This is our little one," he said. Onyx smiled and waved.

"He's such a ham," Montgomery said. "I know they're going to send the hook out here any minute, so I'm going to close. I want to leave you with a few words from my late brother, and then we're out of here.

To navigate the complex realities of the post modern world without compromising yourself requires courage, discipline, and an inquisitive mind capable of great leaps of imagination. In a word—Montgomery!

Montgomery grabbed Zoren and gave him a great big kiss. "Eat your heart out, Ellen!" he said, and they left the stage.

It seems like everybody ended up at the *How to Ruin*…post-Oscar bash. With the movie taking all the top honors including best picture, best screenplay, best actor, best actress and best supporting actress, there was only one place to be.

Jade did a breathtaking surprise performance of her new single *D2,* a tribute to her father and Zoren. The guests went absolutely insane over it.

Her sound was a wonderful blend of jazz rhythms and hip-hop beats. *Rolling Stone* was calling her a cross between Lauryn Hill and Sade, but after her brilliant performance there was no doubt that those comparisons would fall away.

Montgomery and the film's producers took the stage to present a check in the amount of ten million dollars to the newly-formed How to Save a Child Foundation. Montgomery introduced the foundation's Executive Director, Mrs. Gabrielle Johnson, to thunderous applause, and invited her to the stage to accept the check.

Gabby had been floored when Montgomery had called her and beseeched her to take the post. She had relocated to New York and was enjoying the success of her new gallery and her newlywed status as Mrs. Rico Johnson. Montgomery had told her that she was the perfect person to run the foundation and that, if necessary, it could be based in New York, if that's what was required for her to say yes.

As Gabby made her way to the stage, something happened that no one expected—Aprielle walked in.

About the Author

Antonio Le Mons, Michigan State University alumnus and Detroit native, is a professional speaker, trainer, and personal coach. He is currently working on his sophomore fiction project What Becomes of a Legacy, the sequel to How to Ruin the Perfect Child. He resides in Los Angeles and can be reached at HTRTPC@aol.com.

Made in the USA
Monee, IL
10 May 2024

58276861R10142